# SHADOWMEN OBJECTIVE

I0593885

# CURVE

# OF

# HUMANITY

## BOOK TWO

# MAQUEL A. JACOB

Cover art by:

Keith Johnston

Keith Draws

https://keithdraws.wordpress.com


Published by MAJart Works

www.majartworks.com

Hillsboro, Oregon


©Copyright 2016

ISBN: 978-0-9979564-4-3

# ACKNOWLEDGEMENTS

Thank you for taking a chance on my new six book series Curve of Humanity. My great passion is to find the good in humanity and show we can combat corruption within our societies. This book series is a lesson of hope in the face of futility.

Or so I would like to think.

For those who encouraged me to keep going when it all seemed too daunting, I appreciate you all. To the early stage beta readers, Monica Callahan, and Mom, my sincere condolences and immense gratitude. Your enthusiasm and no holds barred feedback is priceless.

A huge thanks to NaNoWriMo (National Novel Writing Month) for supporting writers' creative juices. My peeps at NIWA, you all keep my humble and showed me to put myself out there with no fear.

Sarah Walker and John Howard, two awesome writing buddies who helped hone my craft along with Sean Hoade (you're a hot mess and I love you dearly). Voss Foster, you rock for helping me out in a pinch.

To Jason V. Brock for making me turn the dial in my brain and retrain it. Sunni Brock, you are a ray of sunshine. Thank you, William F. Nolan for constantly telling me not to quit; to keep writing and keep learning.

KEITH JOHNSTON: You are a talented artist. I love how your brain works. The covers turn out amazing. Can't wait to work with you again on future projects.

# ONE : PAVING A WAY

A Sonnet for Humanity

**-Blind Sheep-**

*I had hope for some sense of sanity*
*It being the 21st century of man*
*But, it seems we are losing our humanity*
*With no way of fixing it- If we can.*
*The end is near, or so they say*
*They, being the prophets and pessimists*
*Salivating at the promise of doomsday*
*Even as society and everyday life persists.*
*Let us not fall in line*
*Marching towards our own annihilation*
*And read into the inevitable sign*
*Of our final destination*
*Lest we forget an important note*
*We all wear the same human coat.*

*- Rachel E. Robinson 2012*

## JOINT EFFORT

To the scientists in the room, Aliens were no longer special. For General Roberto Perrara of the United States of America they were the enemy lying in wait, ripe for exploitation. Two security guards escorted him down the white corridors of the Bi-Genetic research facility. A glorified underground torture chamber for hybrid children with alien DNA.

At forty-eight, he had become one the youngest generals in the country and hadn't age a day since being inoculated with alien chromosomes. In his dress blues with immaculately coifed hair and clean shaven, he could easily pass for mid-thirties. His hat tucked under one arm, he tapped the commlink on his wrist.

"To what do I owe this honor?" The older male voice on the other end asked impatiently.

"Professor, I have something quite good to discuss with you."

"Is that so?"

"Let's meet. Say next week?"

"You're coming to Tokyo?"

"I think this will need a face to face."

"Oh?" This time the man sounded intrigued. "I'll have my assistant, Hana, let you know."

"See you soon, then."

He tapped his wrist again to disconnect and found his escorts had led him all the way to the front exit. Daylight lingered, the sun not yet setting.

Outside of Facility Three, he looked up and glimpsed an alien ship hovering above off in the distance. Nearly fifty years had passed since one of the Karysilan race's battle fleet crash landed on Earth. He still couldn't get used to the fact that aliens not only existed but bred with humans to create a newly evolved species. All this in his lifetime.

The meeting with Facility Three's director, Dr. Bartley, along with his personal team of doctors, scientists and engineers rejuvenated Perrara's Professor Makoto's plans to move forward. The scientist had been one of the first to encounter the aliens. With his colleagues combined weight, they overthrew the world governments and took charge of everything crash related.

Over time, when it became apparent that scientists lacked the skill set to run countries or unite them, the military stepped in. The two were still trying to work together while undermining each other. This is what the world looked li.ke now, and it needed a remedy.

The flight to Tokyo took half the time in the newly built commercial jets that defied speed. Instead of using a government convoy, he flew commercial. In coach, no less. General Perrara was at ease during the travel since he had been a fighter pilot back in his early years of the military. The landing left little to be desired, and he had a mind to chastise the pilot for such sloppy handling. He curbed that urge and debarked with the rest of the passengers. He retrieved his bag at the luggage claim, then went outside to grab a town car. As he got in, the Asian driver turned around.

"Where to?"

"You speak English."

"Comes with the territory. Most of the people are

from America these days."

"Is that right? I have a meeting at the Imperial Plaza."

The driver raised an eyebrow.

"Well, let's not keep the emperor waiting."

He turned back around to put the vehicle in drive.

When they arrived at the sixty-story building, Perrara paid with his card and added a thirty-five percent tip. He walked into the reception hall and Professor Makoto's personal assistant, Hana, greeted him. A beautiful young Asian man with chestnut colored air and green eyes. He was also a Bi-Genetic who had been through hell and back inside a corrupt facility in the far countryside.

"General Perrara! It's good to see you again." He grabbed his hand to shake it.

"You're looking well. How's the Professor holding up?"

"Better than most. Come, he's dying to know why you're here."

The two of them got on the private elevator and rode up to Professor Makoto's office suite on the top floor. When it opened, he saw the man himself sitting at his desk, head laid back against the headrest, with his eyes closed. Long hair, pulled tight in a ponytail, had gone completely grey decades ago. Hearing them come in, he sat up and took a deep breath before opening his eyes.

"General, what brings you here so urgently?"

They clasped each other's hands.

"Oh, just a little news about our joint venture we discussed some time ago."

Professor Makoto stiffened at that. Then his face became jovial.

"Sit! Tell me."

The General laughed and set his cap on the desk before leaning back leisurely.

"It is a go, my friend."

Professor Makoto let out a yell, raising his arms in

the air like a school kid at a rally. It was unbecoming of someone his age. Perrara understood how he felt. The time to change the course of humanity was now within reach.

General Perrara and Professor Makoto squared off across from each other at a fold-out table in an emptied hangar. Their vision of a new sector in military might was about to come to fruition after waiting three years for the green light. They still couldn't believe that aliens were on Earth, a part of their population, and there was a new generation of humankind. Professor Makoto, and his fellow scientists, gave hybrids the moniker Bi-Genetics based on the vast majority's ability to shift their sexual orientation at will.

They would now become an intricate part of their project; A new organization that would serve as a cross check for military and government, answering to none. It included every branch from law enforcement to elite soldiers and ghost agents. General Perrara smiled. His own personal faction to mold as he pleased and all from an idea Professor Makoto pitched him some years ago.

Technology had advanced so fast that many sectors around the world couldn't keep up. A hodge podge of old and new riddled the dawn of the 21st century. There were still no hovercraft vehicles in mass production. That didn't apply to the world leaders or the new organization. They had the most toys and the rest of the world wasn't allowed to play with them. No sharing.

Governments around the world had already implemented inhuman regulations regarding the newly hybrid humans. With an alien enemy ready to finish their fight regardless of how Earth ends up in the crosshairs, the Bi-Genetics were slated to become bio-weapons.

Add on top of the aliens' declaration of war, enemy

soldiers had also infiltrated Earth. Discovered sleeper cells found many of them taken to liking Earth and not wanting to see it destroyed, which was lucky for humans. Cooperation from other aliens came slowly but surely. Earth needed all the help it could get.

"My contact at the facility assures me these children on the list are the cream of the crop. Their DNA is optimal for our project." General Perrara drummed his fingers on the table, deep in thought, before continuing. "I'm sure you can handle the rest."

Professor Makoto nodded slowly.

"All that's left is for Captain Darnizva to hold up his end of the deal."

The General pursed his lips. Captain Darnizva commanded the fleet that crash landed so long ago. By his own people's standards, he was a young pup. Nonetheless, he took responsibility and coordinated a joint defensive front. The Captain didn't care for Perrara and Makoto's new venture they both persuaded him to back.

Four aliens from different races had agreed to come to Earth and train the new elite soldiers handpicked by the General and the Professor. They would assign each candidate an area designated for their strengths. The true elites would be taken as children and molded over the course of two decades. Right on target for the impending war.

"Have you seen a dossier on these new aliens?" Perrara asked.

"Nothing yet. I think even Darnizva may not know who is coming until they arrive."

"I have to tell you, I am not a big fan of surprises at this junction."

"Neither am I."

They scanned the hangar, imagining what equipment it would hold. General Perrara hoped for a strategy room while Professor Makoto longed for state-of-the-art communications. The room was one of hundreds within the installation. It could house thousands and the services on site were capable of handling the load.

"Now, how are we going to keep this from getting out to our constituents?"

Professor Makoto grinned. He walked over to the end of the table and sat down in a chair.

"I was thinking of maybe hiding it under another branch that's doing well despite its horrendous attributes."

"Ah," General Perrara said, nodding. "Hoskins."

"Even though he is on the run, the world leaders still kept it running."

"Yes, Terence couldn't absorb every soldier inside."

"It's disgusting, what Hoskins' created."

"And we are going to do much worse."

Professor Makoto's head shot up.

"This will be different!"

The silence inside the heavily insulated hangar weighed down on them. It was no secret how harsh and crude recruitment would be for the greater good. Unlike General Hoskins who hated Bi-Genetics with such passion he constantly put them in harm's way on nearly impossible to win battlefields.

"Well, let's get started." General Perrara scooped his cap off the table and set it right on his head, making sure not to mess up his hair. "No need in delaying our movement."

"Yes." Professor Makoto sighed and stood up.

As they walked to the open steel double doors, a smile crept on both their faces.

A large file sat ready to be opened on the computer screen. Squinting, Professor Makoto's personal assistant, Hana leaned forward and read the size; 4 TB.

*That's a lot of data.*

Hana reached over and grabbed his glasses from the other side of the screen. His vision was not so good these days after the testing rounds happened some years ago. He shuddered. Thinking about it made him remember the excruciating pain of nearly all his bones breaking. Professor Makoto had been livid, cursing everyone in the room. He smiled at that. The professor really did care for him.

When he first heard about the project, Hana felt ill. Another government run killing field for Bi-Genetics. The Professor explained the objective, and he became more at ease with it. Except for the training part. There was no telling what the aliens had in store. He saw the feed of Lieutenant Sspark of the League's attempt at training humans to do alien like maneuvers. It was close to a bloodbath. A football field of carnage.

On the flash drive were folders of each potential candidate compiled into the one file. Hana took a deep breath and double tapped the icon with his fingertip. Data populated the three monitors before him and he used his fingers to swipe them around into an order he liked. He gave priority to the ones already in military service with less than two years, the oldest of them at the ripe age of twenty-five. The aliens would train the first round who become trainers themselves for the new recruits.

He heard the office door hiss open, so looked over to see who had come in. Professor Makoto walked in and stood by him and took in the info on the screens.

"How's it coming along?"

"I just got started," Hana replied defensively.

It came out sounding pouty.

Professor Makoto tilted his head back and chuckled.

"Sorry," he said after. "You know you can't pull such a thing off."

Hana really did pout this time.

"Take me seriously."

"I do." Professor Makoto stroked the top of Hana's head. "You're so adorable."

Hana smacked his hand away and folded his arms in defiance. The Professor laughed again before clearing his throat.

"So, what do you think, really?"

"Too many," Hana replied.

"Hmm. Do you need help sorting through all of this?"

"Absolutely not!" Hana frowned.

"Then what is your solution?"

"Their DNA aside, how well do they perform? I would like to see them in some sort of obstacle course that encompasses every angle."

Shock and excitement spread on the Professor's face.

"That is…" Professor Makoto stepped closer to the monitors. "Genius!" He took hold of Hana and drew him into his embrace. "This is why I adore you." With that, he planted a kiss on Hana's lips.

"But, we don't have anything like that," Hana protested as they disengaged.

"Oh, that won't be a problem. General Perrara would love nothing better than to create one."

Professor turned and walked towards the door. As it opened, and he called out.

"I'll make sure to let him know you came up with the idea."

Back alone in the office, Hana smiled.

*Damn right!*

He may be pretty, but smarter than his looks conveyed.

Inside the underground bunker, General Perrara surveyed every inch of it before giving his analysis. The suggestion of an indoor assessment was indeed right up his alley. With human enhancement through alien DNA introduction, many of the soldiers had heightened senses and could move at fast speeds. He wanted a place to showcase those skills. At some point, he would have to make his way to Tokyo with a gift for Hana. Everyone always underestimated the beauty, forgetting that he was a Bi-Genetic.

Perrara supervised the installation of the bullet and soundproof walls. There were no other buildings in the vicinity. Better safe than sorry. Each piece was enormous and weighed close to five hundred pounds. The workers struggled to hold them in place while they were being riveted.

No need for anyone to hear what's going on, even in the distance.

"Sir?"

A soldier came up to him out of breath.

"What is it, son?"

"We have incoming."

General Perrara smirked, then frowned.

"Explain, soldier."

"Looks like a hovercraft, sir."

"Lock it down, for now," he instructed the workers.

Everyone scrambled to secure their materials, then left the area. With the steel doors shut tight, Perrara headed out to greet whoever sped towards the structure. Outside, he stood at the gate entrance waiting for verification from their visitor. Instead of one hovercraft, there were four. They had been in a single line formation earlier to throw off the lookout. He sucked in a breath as he recognized the man sitting at the helm of the first hovercraft.

"Hoskins. You son of a bitch," he said to himself.

The vehicle halted a few hundred feet away and Perrara's men drew their weapons. Much to his chagrin, Hoskins' entourage spilled out of the other vehicles and did the same.

"General Perrara," Hoskins spat. "Imagine finding you out here in the middle of nowhere in one of my buildings."

"Your building? I think not. This was government property that I happened to get clearance to use for my own personal project."

Hoskins turned red in the face.

"This was mine to house the Terrors when I saw fit!"

"Yes, but you're forgetting something."

"Huh?"

"I could take you in right now and hand you over to the president. He's dying to have a long talk with you." He drew out the word long.

"Hmph. That spineless prick. No one is taking me in." He nodded to his men up front and they surrounded the entrance.

Perrara shook his head in disbelief and made a push down motion with his hand to signal his own men to hold position.

"What are you using my bunker for?" Hoskins paused, "General."

"Nothing you need to know about."

The sound of choppers filled the air, and they all looked up to the sky. Four assault planes packed to the gills with ammo came into view.

"I suggest you take your leave, Hoskins."

"My title is General. You better address me as such."

"I would have to respect you first."

One chopper landed on the far side of the building. Armed soldiers came running out towards them.

Hoskins hissed before backing up.

"I will find out what you're up to." He pointed at Perrara. "Mark my words."

He turned around and double timed it to his hovercraft. All four sped off at the same moment the soldiers reached the gate.

"Do you want us to pursue and capture, General?"

"No." Perrara sighed and gazed at the clouds of dust blocking Hoskins' retreat. "His time'll come soon enough."

Hoskins took another look back as the bunker grew smaller in the rear-view window. True, he had not taken possession of the installation while still in good standing with the government. There was also no clause that said they could strip it from him without notice. Of course, the President had it in for him these days. No one could touch him because of all the information he knew. As one of the first people in the United States to greet the aliens when they surfaced, his country didn't deny him much. Even as he created his Terror squads, not a soul blinked an eye and told him he couldn't.

One of those little monsters named Terence raised a revolt, taking more than half of his comrades with him. Hoskins didn't have a chance against them and now they had their own little facility that no one seemed to get access to. The Terrors he had left were getting uppity, so he had to resort to stronger punishments. That part of the equation is what he needed the bunker for.

He heard about his being taken into custody if found and laughed it off. As he thought, Perrara didn't have the balls to try taking him by force. Not with the four Terrors he had with him as bodyguards. He was sure Perrara noticed which ones they were.

And the President. That sniveling wuss. He'd like to see the man come after him. Teach him a thing or two.

"Where to now, sir?" The driver asked.

Hoskins thought about it for a moment, then a hideous grin formed. He rubbed the bottom of his chin for a moment before snapping his fingers.

"Those fuckers need supplies and getting them somehow." He slapped the soldier next to him with the back of his hand. "Call that snitch and have him research all the known warehouses our private government contractors use."

"Sir?"

"Whatever shady business he's up to, there's no way the big brass would let him ship through government channels."

The soldier pulled out a burner phone and hit a speed dial associated with a secured number. It rang twice, then picked up.

"The General wants you to find the rat holes some rent-a-cops used to fill with goods."

"On it," the voice on the other end replied.

"And don't forget to send me a map," Hoskins yelled.

"Yes, sir," the man said.

The phone went dead, and the soldier turned the phone off.

"Oh, I keep my word, Perrara. I'll take you down and have you begging for mercy."

Hoskins burst into laughter, scaring the soldiers in the vehicle with him. They stared at him in astonishment.

Facility Three was unusually quiet today.

Dr. Bartley stood in front of the large bay windows of his personal quarters that overlooked the entire lab floor. In the cafeteria, he saw the children eating silently. The testing areas off to the right were nearly empty, so the techs lounged at their desks.

Below him, the vidscreen displayed hundreds of files overlapping each other. Every picture represented a

Bi-Genetic his scientists had registered at birth to keep track of their population. He had sent it to Professor Makoto after a year and a half of hard deliberation.

The children in his facility were dear to him. Each facility built for all the wrong reasons. He refused to house government barbarians hell bent on abusing Bi-Genetics. Humans had split themselves into two camps; Regular and Evolved. It was asinine. He himself was a Bi-genetic capable of shifting his gender. Instead, he chose not to, using his position as a facility owner and talent as a scientist to make it better for his kind in the world. Knowing that he had alien DNA still seemed unreal to him.

What Professor Makoto explained to him sounded frightening, yet hopeful. The facilities would be the fail-safe if the plan went awry after implementation. Fifty years was not a long time to prepare for war with an alien race far more advanced than humans could imagine. With decades of science fiction under their belt, none of it compared to the real deal.

He looked down at the vidscreen and began to swipe through them with one finger. Some candidates didn't even know they were a hybrid species, like him back in the beginning. Remembering the experiments inflicted on him made his face scrunch up with hate.

*One day, I'll kill that bastard.*

Shaking his head, he cleared his thoughts and focused on the files. Once the selections were complete and assigned, he had to be ready for his side of the project's initiation.

〰

Neo Tokyo spread wide below General Perrara as he stood at the floor to ceiling windows of Professor Makoto's office. Dusk was nearing. They made a preemptive toast with the twelve-year-old scotch he kept hidden in his desk drawer before their reservation at a five-star restaurant downtown.

"You wouldn't believe who paid me a visit last week." Perrara turned to look at the Professor, his nearly empty glass dangling casually from his fingers.

"In the middle of nowhere?" Makoto frowned as he took a sip of his drink.

"Hoskins."

Professor Makoto sputtered, liquid flying out of his mouth.

"What?"

"Apparently the bunker I requisitioned was one he used for his little army."

"I don't understand why your president doesn't get rid of him."

"Because he knows too much, and we like to keep our enemies close."

Perrara drained the rest of his glass and set it down on the desk. Makoto did the same and stood up.

"Still. He's dangerous. How much do you think he knows about our project?"

"Absolutely nothing," Perrara replied proudly.

"He could find out somehow."

"Then we have failed before our endeavor begins. If we can't keep the organization secret, there's no reason to call it such."

"Ah, noted." Professor Makoto headed for the door. "Come. We have to celebrate."

"No Hana?" Perrara raised his eyebrows

"Did you want him to join us?"

"Of course. I must thank him properly."

Professor Makoto pulled his tablet from his jacket and touched an icon. Two rings sounded, and the line picked up.

"Hana, are you hungry?"

⌇

A group derived from the best spies on the planet converged on the bunker, forming a semicircle of vehicles around the front gate. They totaled nearly one hundred with five to six people per car. Blindfolds covered each one for the trip and none made any complaint about it. Because of their professions, they knew it came with the territory.

On the other side of the gate, General Perrara stood waiting for incoming. He had set up separate briefing rooms for when they ushered groups into assigned sectors. These elites were going to be the organization's observers. Combat would be only when necessary since he brought them for their minds and intelligence. He figured this many would be a great start and could always add more if needed. They would have their fingers on the pulse of everything involved to ensure it all went smoothly.

The doors of all the vehicles opened, and the spies led out in a single file through the main entrance. Some of them tilted their heads, others sniffed the air. Their body language suggested they were trying to get a feel for the location. One man had a wide grin.

"I know that smell. The desert is nice this time of year."

"At least there's air conditioning in this installation. Those units are humming along pretty good," a woman not far down from him added.

Perrara laughed inwardly. He expected nothing less from the handpicked candidates. The soldiers at the gate scanned the barcode each person wore on their wrist.

Hana, in his infinite wisdom, had also suggested the protocol for checking them in. If Professor Makoto hadn't already claimed the beauty, he would have seriously thought about taking him.

He walked over to the soldier right inside the bunker and got close.

"Make sure you leave the blindfolds on, even after they are secured. I don't want them to know anything until the time is right."

"Absolutely, sir. Are we going to give them some refreshments?"

"Now, how would it look if we denied people a drink in the middle of the desert?"

"Very good, sir. I'll get right on it."

As the soldier handed off his clipboard to his counterpart, General Perrara turned his attention back to the line of spies.

*Welcome to a new era of counter intelligence.*

The two spies sat side by side at a table in a small holding cell. Both leaned over, taking a sniff at the glasses full of clear liquid placed before them, and smiled. They raised their glasses and toasted in unison.

"Prost!"

"Salud!"

The glasses, now empty, they slammed down on the table. Perrara gave them a round of applause as he sat in the chair across from them. He removed the manila folder from under his arm and set it down in front of him.

"I hope that was to your liking. I sprung for the good stuff."

"I've had better, but it was still good," the Russian said.

"Not bad. Though I would have preferred some water," the Italian female replied.

"Vodka is water," the Russian protested.

"So." The woman adjusted in her seat. "Are we conducting this interview incognito?"

"My apologies," Perrara said. "I want to make sure you're on board before we talk face to face."

"Understandable. This is something very big if you have spies from all over the world," the Russian stated.

"You could say that." General Perrara leaned forward and rested his forearms on the table. "I, along with Professor Makoto, am creating a new organization that answers to no government. We will be independent yet have power over everything. To do this, we need a network of intelligence that rivals any in the world. Agents who can work behind the scenes, not intervene or change outcomes unless absolutely necessary."

"To what end?" The woman asked.

"To win this war without having humankind becoming extinct." A deep silence filled the room. He continued. "This planet is a board with moving chess pieces. We want those capable of knowing what strategy is required to accomplish our goals."

"Vague, but I like it." The Russian smiled. "I'm in."

"I'm also intrigued. Count my expertise as yours. What are you calling this new order?"

General Perrara nodded to the soldiers guarding the door. They went over and removed the blindfolds. The two spies squinted to adjust their vision in the brightly lit room.

"The Shadow Organization."

He smiled as they also appeared to be amused by the name. He poured another round of vodka, this time one for him as well.

The communication monitor on Perrara's desk lit up with a phone and camera icon. He tapped the touch screen and Professor Makoto's face filled it.

"How did it go?"

"There were only a handful who declined."

"So, we're ready for phase one?"

"Getting the packets together as we speak. Hana is very resourceful."

He saw a hint of possessiveness creep up in the professor's eyes.

"Yes, he is." There was a pause. "What about the training grounds?"

"Still working out the kinks. The indoor assessment looks promising. I believe if even a handful get through that obstacle course, we would have a good unit on our hands."

"Yes, and we need a hell of a lot more than that."

"Don't take me so literally, Professor," Perrara laughed.

It was true, in a sense. They built the course to put a strain on all the senses. One wrong decision and the candidate could get seriously hurt. He had two medical wings set up on either side to ensure a quick response. But the professor was right. They had to get as many units as possible to plant inside the military ranks.

"Phase Two?"

"Still waiting on Professor Bartley."

He knew what the doctor had been through and cursed the scientist who created the facilities. A lot of horrors happened in those places. None of it for the greater good of humanity. This time, the Bi-Genetics on his list would suffer for one that does. Bartley's hesitation was not surprising.

"He's meticulous. Give him all the time he needs. He knows the deadline."

"I'm just anxious," Professor Makoto snapped.

"So am I. Let's have a little more patience."

Professor Makoto nodded.

"I hope to hear an update soon."

With that, the screen went blank and his screen saver resumed. General Perrara sighed and swung around in his chair to face the window. Night had fallen, and the desert sky was full of stars. Mankind wanted so badly to reach further than their solar system. He wondered if that was the right answer, knowing what's out there. Compared to the aliens in their midst, humans were like insects. And not the resourceful kind.

*Can we even win?*

⌒

Professor Bartley sat down at the conference table in the middle of an all-white lab room. Everything in it was white: the walls, the chairs, the floor. His staff of scientists and doctors filed in and took their seats around the table, notebooks and tablets in hand. The issue at bay was the selection process to keep the Bi-Genetic population at a high level. Already, they accounted for twenty-five percent of humans. In another twenty to fifty years, it could reach sixty.

"Good morning, everyone," he greeted them. He received a lackluster reply. "I know you're all tired from your duties, but this is also part of it."

"Yes, we do know." Professor Vasence said.

"It's still a bit scary. Matching candidates with ideal mates based on DNA compatibility for some shady government project." Dr. Harris added.

"Not shady, Shadow." Professor Vasence chastised.

"Whatever. Smells rotten to me."

"That's not so," Bartley interjected. "If done right,

we'll be able to see a light at the end of the tunnel."

"That is contingent on the world governments not mucking it up." Dr. Yan quipped.

"So." Professor Bartley began. "How far have we gotten?"

"About thirty percent. We had to narrow down the potential mates." Dr. Harris replied.

"Maybe we should reinstate a new breeder program?" Professor Vasence asked.

Many of the staff reared back in disgust at the suggestion. That part of Bi-Genetic history was never to be repeated. It was a nasty business that no one was proud of.

"I did say a new one. More humane, perhaps?"

"Let's not and say no." Dr. Harris said as he frowned.

"What is the fail-safe for this plan?" Dr. Yan brought the conversation back on track.

"If everything goes to shit, they can activate a protocol that puts the facilities in a position of power over the governments."

There were gasps, then silence. Every little sound from the equipment in the room seemed to grow louder as time passed, with no one speaking. Finally, a doctor broke the mood.

"That would be ideal now." Dr. Harris said.

"We have to wait our turn," Professor Bartley replied. "Let's see how they do first."

"Hmph. The scientists dove into madness, then the military made a roaring mess. We can't trust these two. They are part of those factions." Dr. Yan scoffed.

"They're different. You, of all people, should know how they feel. And, Darnizva concurs."

"Darnizva has a guilty conscience." Professor Vasence stated.

"Even so, I think we can get this wrapped up within a year's time and help them move on to phase two."

"Aren't we phase two?" Dr. Harris asked, looking around, confused.

"No. That is the frightening part of the project I want no part of. The less we know about what it entails, the better."

"What in god's name are we getting into?" Dr. Yan demanded.

## ALIEN ELITES

On the far side of the moon, stars swirled in an invisible vortex. As it grew, light shimmered around its edges, making the vortex come to life in a brilliant display of color. From its gaping mouth, a large ship cruised forward. Sleek metal with creamy tones covered the underbelly and the back end curved down, forming a tip. As it fully emerged from the vortex, the ship maneuvered sideways at a forty-five-degree angle. The vortex collapsed on itself, shutting the pathway. Veering off, the ship cloaked itself and headed for Earth.

From the helm of his ship, Captain Darnizva watched the alien ship enter Earth space and signaled his crew to prepare for interception. When the President of the United States seemed to be at a loss for methods of training, Darnizva sent out a blanket communication to ask for assistance. He wasn't sure which race had answered his call. They would need basic knowledge of humans before he could let them land on the planet. It shouldn't have come to this.

When he fled the front lines during their battle with Rellia, he assumed the random coordinates would throw them into dead space. Somewhere they could recuperate until help arrived. It still boggled his mind that Rellia's forces tracked them down and involved humans in their fight. For the past few decades, he stayed on Earth to learn more and figure out a way to help. His father was none too pleased about the whole situation.

"Ship is docking, Captain," his second in command announced.

"Good. Let's go see who our new allies are."

Both walked to the lift chamber and his second in command entered the code for the docking bay level. Neither spoke during the ride. This was not an ideal plan, and Darnizva had reservations. His second felt even more uneasy about it. For all they knew, it could be a race far worse than Rellia coming in the guise of help to conquer. If that were the case, Darnizva would take them down before too long. The lift stopped, and the door opened to a hangar bustling with action. His soldiers were getting into position around the vessel, ready for any hostile intent. Cold smoke blew out from beneath it as the exhausts vented.

The bay doors of the ship opened to extend its ramp for the occupants to make their way down. There were four of them, and judging by their attire, two each from different races. Darnizva noticed what planet they came from immediately. Warrior clans. Chombrazens, known for their ground combat and Estelarians for aerial techniques. Similar races divided by two planets. The lone female Estelarian demeanor suggested possible royalty. Her counterpart had an air of being one of her many mates.

*This could get interesting.*

"Darnizva, child. What mess have you gotten yourself into?" She cooed at him.

Her dark blonde hair was a cascade of deep waves that framed her face like a lion's mane. Silver eyes bore into him and he had to actually look up a bit when she came to stand in front of him. The floor length coat made of different animal furs added bulk.

"Trust me, this is not what it seems. Rellia chased us

all the way here. It's their fault."

"No." The Chombrazen on the left said. His deep voice boomed. "You shouldn't have run."

Darnizva balled his hands into fists and clamped his mouth shut.

"Oh, now, don't antagonize the young one," the female said. "I'm sure he had no other choice."

"Yes, he did. Stay and fight…and die if need be."

The female placed a hand on Darnizva's cheek and caressed it before removing her hand.

"He's just a child, really. Stop being cruel. We are here at his behest."

"And I thank you for coming." Darnizva bowed his head to them.

"So, young one. I feel you want to brief us on this world before we go see for ourselves."

"That's correct. More of a warning. They are not…" Darnizva struggle for the right word and came up with nothing.

"Barbarians, are they?" The female's mate asked.

"No, not that. They're just," he paused. "Misguided."

"Oh." The female deadpanned. "This will be an uphill battle then."

"In every way."

After a month of debriefing the fresh addition of aliens, Darnizva loaded them up in his convoy ship and accompanied them down to Earth for a meeting with General Perrara. For some reason, he was very nervous. What if they didn't get along? Would he have to extinguish a bloody fight? He glanced over at the female Estelarian, Telia. She was always smiling. On her left, the second, smaller Chombrazen, Lindo, sat brooding. His face scrunched up as if concentrating on something.

During the talk sessions, he could see the disdain

creep up in their expressions. Humans were quite inferior and knowing they had to co-mingle with them left little to be desired. Darnizva didn't blame them one bit. He had seen and experienced enough of humankind to almost feel the same, although he knew not all humans were bad.

"What is this General like?" The bigger Chombrazen, Karias, finally asked.

"Very dedicated to his cause. A true military man who thinks before taking action."

"Yet, he is only one in a sea of plenty." Telia added.

"You'll see. He has conviction."

"That doesn't win battles," Karias snapped. His partner gave him a sideways glance.

The rest of the flight was in silence until they reached the bunker in the middle of the desert. Telia's mate, Attar, was the first to speak as they stepped out into the dark of night.

"What a barren place."

"We're trying to keep it secret, so location was key," Darnizva explained.

"There are better ways."

Four armed soldiers appeared at the gate entrance and snapped to attention. From the open doors came General Perrara, his uniform impeccable along with his hair. Darnizva smirked. The man's vanity never ceased to amaze him. Always a charmer, the General gave his most winning smile and went straight for the female warrior.

"Please to see you have arrived safely. I am General Perrara from the United States of America. Welcome to Earth."

He took her hand and kissed it, bowing as he did so. Her mate unsheathed his weapon. General Perrara raised an eyebrow and the female warrior burst out into laughter.

"Have I offended you in some way?"

She stopped laughing and shook her head, the movement of her hair mesmerizing.

"Not at all. My mate likes to appear territorial."

"He's doing a good job."

Attar put back his weapon and stepped back.

"The United States. One of the so-called super-powers." Karias folded his arms. "Yet, you have showed poor leadership."

"I can't argue with you there. But," Perrara raised a finger. "I am trying to remedy that."

"All by yourself? You are just one human," Attar cried out.

"It only takes one to change the fate of an entire race."

General Perrara smiled wide, and turned towards the bunker. Darnizva figured out what that expression was; elation.

The four aliens surveyed the bunker and took in every aspect of each section as the general guided them. Perrara beamed with pride while explaining his ideas on how the training set up should work. Only a tenth of the equipment and materials needed were on hand. Darnizva also made his own observations of the bunker. In his mind, the facility itself seemed primitive. By human standards, it was top of the line. He knew with certainty that the aliens would bring in their own technology to help along.

At a wall of double doors spanning twenty feet wide and even higher height, Perrara entered a code on the side panel. A small platform slid out, and he placed his right hand on it. A red light scanned it, then a green light flashed. The doors made a loud whirring sound before hissing from released pressure and opened, sliding to either side. Strong wind came through, nearly pushing them all back, the smell of scorched desert air assaulting their nostrils.

"Come. You must see our natural terrain."

They stepped out onto a platform that set atop a mountain cliff and on the other side, down below was a massive forest, green and lush.

"How?" Darnizva whispered as he stood in awe.

"New advances in agriculture let us grow this entire area in mere months. Accelerated synthesis."

"Hmm? That's quite ambitious. Whatever for?" Telia asked.

"Do you not have to know how to defend yourselves in environments such as this?" Perrara responded.

"Ahh. Well, if it somehow comes to that."

"Why wouldn't it?"

"I'm quite sure Rellia will raze the surface so they can see their targets better."

Perrara's face contorted.

"They would have to get a shot off first." His tone was full of anger.

"It would be ideal. The general is correct. And Rellia doesn't have much foliage, so you humans may have a great advantage." Lindo added.

"If that is the case, then is this terrain a suitable size for such training?" Attar asked.

Darnizva visually inspected the forest and knew from firsthand experience it was.

"This is more than adequate, I assure you," he told them.

Perrara cleared his throat to get their attention and gestured towards the doors.

"There is much more to see, of course."

"We can finish the tour at another time," Karias snapped. "Where will our housing be in this place?"

"Yes, a decade or two is nothing if I'm comfortable

in my new environment." Attar said.

Telia gave her mate a knowing glance.

"Of course, that's a great idea," Perrara replied, obviously heartbroken.

He led them through a maze of hallways until they reached a lift nearly the same size as the outer terrain doors. Again, he had to use the same protocols as before to activate it. Inside, there was only one panel. Perrara produced a keycard and swiped it across. The lift doors hissed shut, followed by its descent. It puzzled Darnizva. He wasn't sure the aliens would enjoy being holed up underground. When the doors reopened, he had to admit his surprise.

In front of them spanned a wide-open side view of the forest from the backside of the mountain. They were literally inside of it. The large quarters seemed to go on forever. A lounge area, four vidscreens and every amenity the humans deemed necessary for them was ready for enjoyment.

"How wonderful!" Telia exclaimed.

She walked around doing a 360 turn. The others did the same in opposite directions.

"Each room has a view like this, so you can see the recruits in action and make assessments." Perrara explained. "I know these accommodations must seem small. We want you to be satisfied."

"This is more than enough for a brief stay," Lindo replied.

"There is one more thing," Perrara said. He went over to the closest recess and tapped on the wall. A panel appeared. "This is a hidden lift for only you. It leads to a command center of sorts. Shall we?"

Everyone loaded up in the lift when the panel slid open, and this time they went back up four levels lower than the main. The panel opened to a dark space with hardly anything of value visible.

"This used to be a hangar, so it's in the process of being retrofitting for your needs. Of course, you can reconfigure it as you wish."

The four aliens seemed to smile as they stood staring into the void. Darnizva could tell they indeed had their own plans. He felt a sense of unease. The humans had no idea what they asked for.

⟿

Rain ran down the windows of Professor Makoto's office as he looked down on Tokyo. He loved the rainy season because it cleansed away the horrors. From his view, he could see the people going about their daily lives walking the streets and sitting in cars during traffic. Further out was the facility he had built so long ago to house Bi-Genetics. It still functioned as an intake despite the number of children being tossed away, had dwindled considerably over the past ten years. Hana had come from there and to this day he regretted not overseeing the place better.

A swishing sound made him turn to see Hana coming through the door with a handful of folders. He knew what they were. In order to have more secure briefings, he made hard copies to be destroyed later. Hana seemed jubilant, so he went to help set the folders down while he got himself together to tell him why.

"Guess what?" Hana asked breathlessly.

"Tell me."

They're here!"

Professor Makoto's eyes went wide.

"I got a call from General Perrara while getting these."

"So, it begins."

Makoto sighed and went to sit in his chair.

Hana gave him a perplexed look.

"I thought this was what you wanted."

"It is. I just wish we had implemented this sooner. So much could have been prevented."

"You can't save the whole world, Professor."

"No, but I could at least try."

"Are we going to get to meet them?"

"I would assume so. At least once. After that, we shouldn't have much contact with them."

Hana nodded in acknowledgement. The fact that he understood was a godsend to him. There was no other in his immediate circle who he could share his ideals with.

"Oh," Hana suddenly perked up. "You also wouldn't believe this."

Professor Makoto shifted forward in his seat.

"Professor Morandi left a message for you to contact her. She wants to touch base and see what you're up to these days."

He reared back against his seat. Morandi. That woman always knew too much. As one of the founding members of the new world order after the alien crash, she had a way of keeping her fingers deep in the artery of every Bi-Genetic. The last person he wanted to speak to was her.

"Hana," Professor Makoto started.

"She's a roaring cunt, isn't she?"

Professor Makoto was taken aback by Hana's remark. He simply nodded in agreement.

"And her personal assistant is no better than the people who tortured us in the facilities."

"Yes, well, he has some demons to sort out."

"Are you going to answer her request?"

"Let's make her wait until after we meet our new organization partners."

"That's a much better idea."

As Hana went to work organizing the folders for

the next briefing, Professor Makoto let himself smile a little. He could never have imagined Hana being so free in expressing his feelings and laughing. For so long, the young man seemed frightened all the time, obeying as a defense mechanism from harm. Pushing himself up from the chair, he went over to help.

*My beautiful flower.*

〜

Darnizva had acquired a taste for Human food over the decades. He found himself a carnivore, especially partial to red meat. The steak in front of him still sizzled on the plate with a large helping of mashed potatoes and greens. According to society, this was a 'man's' meal. He sat across from General Perrara. Professor Makoto and Hana were on either side of him. The restaurant was half empty at the General's request.

It had posh carpeting and velvet drapes on the windows. Each table had fine china with equally impressive silverware. The entire staff wore black shirt and pants with white waist aprons for contrast. Every now and again, they would glance over at the table, their curiosity showing.

"So," Professor Makoto began, "Why is it our new friends aren't here to celebrate with us?"

He speared a piece of his broiled fish and slowly placed it in his mouth, savory its flavor.

"I don't think they're ready for that just yet. It would be good to let them settle into their new surroundings for a while," Darnizva replied as he too took a bite of his steak.

The juices lubricated his lips as he chewed and had to admit it was the best steak he had eaten so far. Tender, slightly salty and moist: medium rare. He closed his eyes for a moment, relishing the taste. When he opened them, he saw the rest of his party staring at him. Perrara laughed.

"Is it really that good, Captain?"

Embarrassed, Darnizva set his fork down and used the napkin to wipe his mouth.

"Sorry. Yes, it's that good."

"Then when can we meet them?" Professor Makoto was not about to be led off track in the conversation.

"I figured we could fly out tomorrow," Perrara said.

"Barring any surprise visit, I guess that is acceptable."

Darnizva looked up at Perrara, puzzled.

"What does he mean by that?"

Perrara let out a loud exhale, then set his napkin on the table beside his plate.

"Hoskins."

That name alone made Darnizva's skin bristle. He too wondered why the President didn't just get rid of him. And he didn't mean kill him. Just lock him up and throw away the key. Anything to keep the man on a leash and out of their hairs.

"How did he find out about the bunker?"

"Apparently, he was given permission previously to use it for his Terror Squads. Of course, that permit was rescinded after the last debacle he created."

They all remembered when Hoskins unleashed some new missile and sent it hurling towards the enemy. It only served to piss them off and Earth was nearly blown into oblivion if it wasn't for an unexpected savior.

"You do know he's going to try and dig up any information on what you're doing with it?"

"Oh, I don't doubt that," Perrara smirked.

"Don't forget Morandi," Hana piped in.

Professor Makoto winced.

"Her too?" Darnivza asked.

He scooped up some mashed potatoes with a piece

of steak secured on his fork and shoved it in his mouth.

*So amazing!*

He finished chewing and took a deep breath before speaking. His cinnamon-colored eyes seemed to turn bright red, like the color of fresh blood.

"Let's see how secret you can keep this."

Like a child seeing something extraordinary for the first time, Hana let out a breathless sigh when he saw the four aliens. Especially at the female who stood a good seven feet tall. Her mane-like hair was a giant mound of fluffiness. His hand twitched with the urge to touch it. She bent down so that they were eye level and smiled. Hana actually blushed.

Darnizva sat in a corner observing the interaction and concluded this was a good thing. He wasn't so sure about having Hana at the meet. Professor Makoto just stood to the side, not saying a word. His expression, one of fear and Darnizva couldn't figure out why until he followed the Professor's gaze to the Chombrazen warrior, Karias. There seemed to be no mutual like between them.

"So," Karias' voice boomed. "You are one of the scientists who initiate the travesties we've heard about.

It instantly killed the mood in the room. Hana's face crumbled. The female alien turned towards the warrior with a look of annoyance. The professor seemed prepared to flee. General Perrara stepped into the middle of the room.

"Now, to be clear, he had the best intentions. His colleagues had other plans, and he was overruled."

"Is that your excuse, human?"

He crossed his massive arms in front of him and glared down.

"I have no excuse. You're right. I should have done more." He lowered his head. "Fought more."

"Let's not chastise the one who is at least trying," Telia chided.

"Hmph!" Karias dropped his arms and went to stand at the window.

Telia turned her attention back to Hana.

"Are you going to be one of my students?"

Hana went pale and backed away, shaking his head.

"No?" She stood up to her full height. "Pity. I would make you powerful."

"He's not a plaything," Darnizva said, getting up. "I think we should get down to the task at hand."

Telia grinned.

"We have brought something that should be beneficial. I'm sure your medical science will appreciate it as well."

Her mate opened his palm and a full sized holoscreen spread in midair. The image resembled a cryochamber that laid flat.

"What is it?" Professor Makoto scrutinized the image up close.

"A regeneration chamber," she answered sweetly. That stunned him, along with Hana and the General. "We can't tear them apart and not have a way to repair them, so we can do it all over again."

"Tear apart?" Hana spoke softly.

"Make no mistake. We are not here to coddle your kind. You want to be on equal footing with the races outside your solar system, then death is the way. Once you've been torn apart, pain is inconsequential."

General Perrara pursed his lips while appearing to contemplate something. Meanwhile, Professor Makoto's eyes lit up.

"We can duplicate this technology for medical science?"

"Of course. How else is the human race going to survive through this? We've brought ten of them.

Your scientists can mull over one for research and development."

"Thank you," Professor Makoto stuttered. Tears formed in his eyes. "Thank you, for everything." He bowed his head low in appreciation.

Darnizva didn't know what to think. He knew the aliens would come in having a strict regimen for training the newly evolved humans. Putting them through the brink of death was a bit extreme. His gaze caught that of the other three and he saw glints of anticipation…and malicious intent.

⌒

Sounds of meat being slapped carried out into the parking lot where Hoskins waited in the back seat of his car. The driver read a book, occasionally glancing over towards the noise. After a few more minutes, three men came out of the old warehouse. Their hands were bloody. One of the men handed out wet wipes to clean them off. As they got into the car, the driver set his book down and put the car in drive. It sped off down the gravel road.

"Well?" Hoskins demanded.

"Yeah, the guy said he didn't know much. Just that the bunker was sold to a facility who gave it to your general friend."

"He's no friend of mine, that rat bastard!" Hoskins contained his anger, then it hit him what the thug said. "A facility? Which one?"

"He didn't say. Something really shady is going on. Something about recruiting ghosts."

"That sneaky son of a…" Hoskins stopped and looked down at the men's hands. "Did you kill him?"

"What? Nah! You didn't say that's what you wanted."

"So, you left a witness?" Hoskins yelled.

"Well, not exactly," the second thug answered.

"Huh?" the first said.

From behind, a giant explosion erupted, engulfing the entire warehouse. Everyone in the vehicle flinched except for the second thug. Debris flew up in the air and all the way down the road.

"I don't like loose ends," he shrugged.

Hoskins let out a loud guffaw and slapped his thigh. When he finished, he wiped his eyes and became more serious.

"I told you I'd find what you're up to, sooner or later."

The vehicle sped on, heading towards his new hideout.

⌒

A headache came on and a chill ran through General Perrara. In the middle of the new medical wing inside the bunker, he stood scanning the layout. He checked his surroundings and found no places where air would come in. Professor Makoto looked up from his work, concerned.

"Are you alright?"

"Yeah. Just got a chill."

"In my culture, that means someone is thinking or talking about you."

"That could be anybody."

The doors opened, and a soldier came hustling in, a panic-stricken expression on his face.

"What you got, son?"

"Sir," the soldier barely got trying to catch his breath.

"Take it slow. Tell the situation."

A giant gut bomb landed in his stomach as he braced for impact.

"Some hard asses ambushed one of our guards. They poured gasoline all over him and the floor. The warehouse and everything in it is destroyed."

"The supplies?"

"Gone, sir."

"Our man?"

"You won't believe this. Someone else must have been in there watching, cuz we found him a good ways away from the building. He's burnt a bit."

"Where is he now?"

"On his way to the nearest burn unit."

"Reroute him!"

"Sir?"

"Get him here." Perrara turned to Professor Makoto. "They showed you how to use those things, right?" He turned back to the soldier. "Who were these men?"

The soldier grew angry. His bottom lip quivered while his hands balled into fists.

"The guard said one name."

Perrara and Makoto both sucked in air through their teeth. The soldier didn't need to say who it was.

"That son of a ..." they exclaimed in unison.

Then what the soldier said before that clicked in Perrara's head. Someone was watching. And not interfering unless necessary. A sense of relief came over him. The program was in play.

Some days, were more productive than others and today was one of those. Shipments came flooding in through the bunker all hours of the day. Every crew worked overtime to get orders where they needed to go. It had taken three months to replace the materials lost in the warehouse fire, throwing the timetable off track. The aliens seemed unfazed by it, building their own comforts in the command center.

Hana was overseeing placements in each sector to ensure equipment installation went without a hitch. He made it clear to General Perrara and the Professor that he would not tolerate being disturbed from his duties.

There was just too much to do and not enough time. Recruitment was going to start within weeks and they had to be ready.

"Excuse me, sir," a soldier called out to him. He blushed at 'sir'.

"What is it?"

"The electricians are here to set up all the cameras and monitors."

"Oh, good. Escort him to the holding areas first."

"Roger that, sir."

The soldier left, and Hana giggled a little before regaining his posture. The recruits would have no privacy whatsoever. Every nanosecond of their time spent in training would be documented to correct any flaws in the program. They could be tweaked to make it more efficient. From the timeline, it looked to span nearly thirty years, maybe more. It would put them right at the deadline for battle.

Out of the corner of his eye, he caught sight of the female's mate strolling in the supply room. The alien had a curious look on his face as he perused the goods.

"Looking for anything in particular?" Hana asked as he walked up to him.

Attar turned and scanned his whole body with his eyes, making Hana feel violated. He backed away.

"No. I wondered what all of this is for."

"Well, there are things necessary to sustain basic life, you know."

"Ah, yes. Food, shelter and such. And these?"

He pointed to an open crate full of weapons and ammunition.

"For training purposes. They need to know how to properly defend themselves in our own environment before we can adopt new techniques."

Attar frowned. His eyes bore into Hana's.

"You seem to be very knowledgeable for a human with no combat skills."

"I studied it. If you want to know how we fight, you should too."

He didn't mean it to come out condescending. Attar bristled at him then his demeanor changed.

"Are we getting more acquainted?" Telia asked from afar. As she got closer, her mate seemed to stiffen.

"Of course. Hana was just informing me of the study materials we need to go over before the arrival of our students."

"Is that so?" She towered over them and peered down. "I already have."

Her stare conveyed disgust at the subject and Hana couldn't fault her. Humans were a flawed species capable of horrific levels of cruelty, killing each other on a daily basis. He could tell that she was full of anticipation to see it up close. For the first time, he feared them. The way they acted now solidified in him what they truly were. Another race of beings whose sole purpose was victory over their enemies. Members of a warrior clan far more advanced in combat than even the Karysilans.

After the two aliens left following that terse exchange, Hana walked as fast as he could to the little office he had made for himself to facilitate tasks. Inside, he slumped against the door and leaned hard into it. The tablet he had been carrying fell to the floor and he saw his hands were shaking. As an evolved human with alien DNA he knew he should be stronger, to be able to strike down any opponent and bend them to his will. That was just it. He had the answer to his own riddle.

*I'm not a killer.*

⌒

General Perrara walked along the sterile white halls of Facility Three trying not to breathe in the scent of hopelessness. It appeared to be silent as a tomb while he was being escorted to Bartley's conference room. The last time he was there, the scientists and doctors were not too friendly. Now that his plans had come to fruition, he had better leverage. Each division toiled day and night to get it off the ground. On the tablet he held in one hand as he walked were the different levels of candidates he would require. Matching them up according to Bartley's database was the last step.

He hated being in any of the facilities, and this one was the better of them. Even Professor Makoto's still combated major issues, and people continued to voluntarily give up their children if they showed a hint of Bi-Genetic traits. The number of babies tossed in dumpsters or children found half beaten to death near state lines had dwindled, but not zero.

The two security guards who led him had monster written all over their demeanor. They had certainly done horrible things to their wards in the beginning and probably felt bitter about Bartley stopping that behavior the moment he took over. He could tell neither would have made it in the military and definitely not his training.

They stopped at a solid wall and the one on the left produced a keycard that he swiped downward. Lines formed in the shape of a door, and the panel slid open.

"This way. Watch your step. The lights are motion sensored, so they won't come on until you get further in to trigger them." The one on the right said this as he moved out of the way for the General to proceed.

He walked right into brief darkness until after a few feet, lights flickered. The peach-colored bay came into view and he sped up to a brisk walk.

"Hold up," the left guard yelled. "You need to wait

for us to guide you."

The man's tone made Perrara want to turn and punch him in the face, yet he gathered his composure and forced himself to stop. The quicker he could get through the bay, the less uneasy he would feel. Every window was a lesson in despair filled with children being tested based on their unique talents. Some were telekinetic, while others had more frightening gifts. These were the type of children Hoskins had snatched up for his Terror squads.

At the end of the bay was another panel and this time they ended up back in a white walled environment. He remembered this hall from his last visit. Three conference rooms down, the guards stopped at the entrance and pushed the commlink on the outside wall.

"General Perrara is here for his appointment."

"You are dismissed," a female voice on the other end said. "We can take it from here."

He smirked, knowing that voice well. He could never forget the good doctor. The two guards seemed visibly irritated, as if their authority was being usurped. They turned away and went back to where they came from. As they passed General Perrara, they gave him a dirty look. He smiled at them, then proceeded to the door. It slid open for him and he entered the room.

"Well, you kept us waiting long enough," Dr. Yan said.

Short, fit, and Asian, the doctor made her way to her seat. As usual, she wore her lab coat over a thin blouse and nearly illegal white mini skirt. Her pumps were a staggering five inches to make her seem to be five feet six.

*One day,* Perrara said to himself.

At the table in the middle of the room sat the rest of Bartley's inner circle. There were eight in all, comprised of scientists, engineers and doctors. Bartley sat at the helm, looking weary. His dark wavy hair hung loose, framing his pale face.

He wore slacks and a t-shirt, no shoes.

"General," he greeted him.

"Doctor Bartley. Are you doing well? You seem tired."

"How dare you ask that after what you had him do for your little project," Dr. Yan yelled.

Bartley raised a hand. She fell silent, albeit defiantly. Perrara let out a sigh.

"I assure you, this is no little project, and I have put just as much, if not more, time invested in it."

"Let's just get this over with," an engineer snapped.

General Perrara sat down in an empty seat and placed his tablet and hat in front of him on the table.

"Is everyone going to be testy the whole meeting?"

"No. I won't tolerate it," Bartley answered.

Everyone's demeanor changed to signs of defeat.

Perrara set his tablet in the middle before him, and the sensors caught. A hologram for each folder sprung to life on the device. Scientists on both sides tapped onto the table in front of them and two more came up, making his the middle one.

"So, what's the timeline again?" A scientist asked.

"I want to have the priority ones mated by the time they reach nineteen. Twenty-five would be better."

"That's what we figured. Collating the data now."

The scientist did more tapping on the virtual keyboard that barely lit up when he touched it. All three holograms merged into one and strings of data flowed up like a river. From where he sat, Perrara could see files attaching themselves to personnel files.

"What about the ones already in play?" Another engineer asked.

"I have a special training program for them," Perrara answered. "From our combined lists, I found a good many within the military, law enforcement and hospitals."

"What, no government workers with sorry lives you can ruin?" a doctor retorted.

"I said, I won't tolerate it," Bartley warned.

Perrara swerved in his chair and looked directly at the rude doctor.

"As a matter of fact, I have found a few of those, too."

The doctor frowned and settled back in his chair.

"No stone unturned, huh?" He muttered.

Bartley leaned forward in his seat and rested his elbows on the table. A fearsome look crossed his face as he stared at Perrara.

"I want to reiterate that if this goes badly, we take over the entire thing."

"I wouldn't have it any other way." Perrara gave him a look of assurance.

"Always have a plan B, C, and D," Dr. Yan added.

# CHAPTER TWO : GUIDELINES

## RECRUITMENT

Across from the massive private school housing the offspring for some of the wealthiest, and most crooked, families in society, an observer sat on a park bench pretending to read his tablet. The late summer heat had subsided and a cool breeze swept through, rustling up the few random leaves that had fallen. Children's laughter filled the air as they played in the courtyard. Two of them he kept constant vigil over.

The first boy, Victorrio Marzonetti, was the son of a mafia dom. Tall for his age, with thick dark hair and light brown eyes, he appeared to be very attached to the other target, Eldan. A smaller boy with light blonde hair, fairly skinny and piercing grey eyes that almost looked silver. Whenever the sun caught them, the observer shuddered. Something about him was disturbing.

His parents were renown in the charity circuit as generous philanthropists. Of course, that was all a ruse. They were the most cruel and despicable people in the tri-state area. Neither boy could claim to be exactly upstanding students, either. What could one expect when you grow up with shitty parents or in a life of crime?

Another boy threw a mud ball at Eldan, hitting him in the side of the face. Before he could react, Vic had the little shit by the throat, throttling him. Some of the other kids got between them to break them up. The observer sighed. He wasn't sure if putting them in the same training sector was a good idea.

At one o'clock, a bell tolled, signaling the end of recess. Brushing themselves off, the little darlings headed back into the school. Along the way, they all pushed and shoved, cursing profanities. The teachers said nothing as they passed. He hated children; especially the ones their age. Between ten and twelve, kids thought they were invincible to discipline. He snorted. Those two would learn the hard way.

Shutting down his tablet, he tapped the commlink on his wrist to wake it up, then entered a four-digit code. It would initiate the grab as a go. He would voice his opinion about their training to the upper echelon when he got back to his hideout.

A studio apartment on the fifth floor of an historic building turned housing complex overlooked the town center and beyond that the school. He sat down at his desk and viewed the images flooding across his three touchscreen monitors. One image he tapped and brought to the forefront. That one he knew would be the catalyst to give a window of opportunity. Eldan's parents hated the fact that he was a Bi-Genetic. They stressed, beat into him rather, that he kept up appearances by not interacting inappropriately with other boys.

The image showed Vic forcing a kiss on Eldan. That's what happened, yet the picture conveyed otherwise. He found the mother's personal email and attached the image with no message. There was no need to send it to the father as well. Of the two parents, the mother was the most vicious. She would show it to him.

For a slight moment, the observer felt bad for the brat, then he thought about ten, fifteen years from now and that feeling went away. This was all for the sake of humanity. As for the other boy, he sent words of encouragement to the extraction team that had to go into a mafia den to get him. There would be no control of the media in that regard. The situation will look like a rivalry fight.

He checked the time and sat back in his chair to let his head rest. When he was first approached about his new mission, he was hesitant. More than an ambitious venture, it was outright insane. Trying to turn the tide through such drastic means appeared cruel and inhumane. Now, he saw what the General had in mind and was glad he came on board.

His stomach growled.

Sitting up, he contemplated going to the restaurant four blocks down that had a better view of the landscape. Seeing the whole thing go down intrigued him.

Back roads on the outskirts of state lines were a treasure trove of abandoned children if one looked hard enough. Some could be found right along the edge, whereas others were dumped farther in to blend with the overgrown brush. A dark sedan screeched to a stop by the side of the road nearly ten miles past the border. Dusk fast approached with the sun dying fast. Two men came out of the vehicle and scanned the area. There wasn't much time before night set in.

The package had a tiny tracking unit injected unbeknownst to them. The first man looked down at a small screen he held in his hand. A small dot blinked on a map showing it somewhere in the deep tall weeds a good ten yards away. He shook his head in sorrow and turned to his partner. The other man hit the key fob to pop the trunk.

They had witnessed the travesty that ended up here. The family was white collar millionaires with a superiority complex. They schmoozed with the big dogs and made sure they had pictures to prove where they had been. The one thing they didn't do was let their youngest son in on the fun.

His parents kept him prisoner inside the house except for going to school. When the boy finally broke and tried to leave while they were out, the family came back due to a time mess up. The entire horde; mother, father and both brothers took turns delivering blows until he lay still.

It was a lesson in patience and resolve for the two men because they wanted so badly to go in and rescue the boy from his home. In a panic, the family wrapped him up in sheets and drove forty miles to the state border. The men waited until they passed on the way back before going to retrieve him.

As they walked through and found the poorly wrapped bundle, the second man stopped to slap a hand over his mouth. He fought back tears and vomit.

Being an observer meant not interfering with the plans. Sometimes, when they saw things like this, both men questioned their roles.

"Let's get him up gently," the other man said as he stowed the small screen.

The other nodded and removed his hand, regaining his composure. They bent down on either end and carefully lifted the body up. A small hiccup followed by a spurt of blood erupting from the boy's mouth made them stop for a moment.

"I hope you're as strong as you seem, kiddo," the first man said.

They got him into the padded trunk and made sure he was comfortable. The second man took out a handkerchief and wiped the blood from the boy's mouth. He could tell by the boy's position that his arm may be broken. Back in the front seat, the men sat for a while, not talking. Finally, the driver took the wheel and maneuvered the vehicle in a U-turn. It sped down the highway and got off the nearest exit ramp. From there, they got on a junction that would take them to a private airstrip.

A group of boys were playing street hockey in an alleyway on the bad part of town. They usually made the trip from their nice neighborhoods and big houses to seek out and harass the lower class. The alley used to be the playground for another bunch of kids until they came and beat the crap out of them, taking it over. Every now and then, some of the locals would pass by and give them dirty looks, that being the extent of it. Their families had money and even the cops didn't dare touch them.

One boy hit the chunk of plastic too far and it went towards the opening of the alleyway.

"Hey, jackass!" he yelled at the boy next to him. "Go get that."

"Why don't you go get it? You hit it over there." The other boy retorted.

"Cuz, I said so." His family had the most money, so he became their leader somehow.

"Whatever."

The other boy walked down to get the 'puck' while the others started laughing at one of the leader's lame jokes. He knelt over the chunk of plastic and heard screeching. Looking up, he saw a minivan speeding around the corner towards him.

"Hey, what's that?" The leader asked as he headed his way with the others in tow.

Before they could get to him, the minivan lurched to a halt directly in front of him. Two men reached out, grabbed him, and then the vehicle sped off, the sliding door slamming shut as it went. The other boys stood in shock. One of them began yelling, and the leader walked the rest of the way to the alley entrance. He watched the minivan disappear as he fell to his knees, feeling helpless.

"Keep still, you little shit!" The hooded man ordered.

The boy fought hard with everything he had, but the men were twice his size. He became desperate and thrashed about, trying to bite, kick, punch his way out. He didn't know if it was a kidnapping for money or what. His father always told him to make sure to leave a mark if he felt like his life was in danger. This wasn't the first time someone had tried to extort money from his family by doing a snatch and grab. Last time was his sister.

"You have to do it or he's going to keep at it," the driver said.

He didn't even see the fist come at him, only the impact as it hit him in the side of the head. Tiny dots floated before his eyes, disorienting him. Shaking it off, he tried to struggle and was hit again. Then again. His head snapped back, and he felt his limbs go slack. In an attempt to shield himself, he raised an arm. The next blow sent him into oblivion.

Hunched over a container of Chinese takeout, the coordinator took a glance at his holoscreen to confirm the grab. Cameras were inside the sunglasses the operatives wore, so he saw it all go down in real time. He commended the young man for fighting, as he should. There was no way for him to win, and that last hit made even the coordinator wince. It was only acceptable because of his age. At twelve, the boy could take it.

More than a mere observer, he made things happen. Hurting children wasn't exactly his cup of tea. If it was necessary, so be it. The consensus among many of the operatives was their lack of affection for anyone under the age of eighteen. And even that was being generous.

On the screen next to that one, he saw the young boy whose parents dumped him on the side of the road being unloaded from the private jet onto a stretcher. The desert air swirled around him and the two men that brought him. Nurses performed triage during the flight and the broken arm looked to have been reset and resting in a sling. He wondered if the boy would survive. As a grown man, he felt if that were him, he'd beg for death. Maybe commit suicide.

*That's a lie.*

He shook his head, chastising himself for thinking it. He loved life, his life, too much for something as trivial as a royal beat down to do him in.

Using one hand, the coordinator swiped the first screen to the right, pinched it, then dragged it down to the tabletop interface. He double tapped a different feed and brought it up. The house of Dom Marzonetti with its lush garden and exquisite stone structure came into view. Armed men in black surrounded the perimeter. He shoved another mouthful of noodles in his mouth and zoomed in on the son's window. The boy was inside. He typed in a code to the operations leader, giving them the green light.

*This was going to get a little bloody.*

He said to himself.

Word came through about one of the other mafia families not being satisfied with a shipment agreement and that retaliation was in store. Dom Marzonetti sat in his home office, relaxed in his large leather chair, contemplating the news. His top officers were in the room with him and they were all silent. In his mind, it was a trivial matter. If they didn't like the terms, good riddance. Retaliation over it was stupidity on their part. He knew firsthand about that family taking things out of context and doing just that. He figured they wouldn't dare do so with him because his family was equal in size. A fight would be bloody on both sides.

"Well, what's the plan?" He asked his right-hand man.

"I guess we wait and see if they contact us." He replied.

"You really think they're going to negotiate?" His second asked.

"I don't know, their Don is pretty…"

The sounds of machine gunfire and glass shattering cut the conversation short. Don Marzonetti's face grew pink with anger and his officers pulled out their weapons. Protecting the head was their first priority.

"Get my son!"

His head enforcer, Bartoni, nodded and headed out the door, cautiously looking left, then right, before easing out. The other enforcer slammed the door shut and waited for any action to come their way.

Bartoni moved through the house as stealthily as possible, dodging stray bullets that came flying all around. His own crew moved around trying to take down a few with not much success. Out of the corner of his vision, he glimpsed the enemy. Black suits and ski masks. A glint of light caught the metal pins of the family insignia. He frowned. It was theirs alright, although something about their movements seemed too…fluid.

He reached the upper level of the house and headed for Vic's room, only to run right into a group of the enemy. They immediately fired on him, missing as he leaped sideways out of their line of sight. The wall across from Vic's room turned into Swiss cheese. He thanked his lucky stars it wasn't him. Shaking debris from his head, he got to his hands and knees. Just as he was about to scramble for cover, a click sounded in his ear. He turned and saw one of the enemy standing over him, gun cocked and aimed straight at his temple. Brown eyes were the only thing visible from the mask and there was no malice in them.

"Sorry, guy. We can't let you stop us and we can't let you go."

He pulled the trigger, three in succession, and Bartoni felt each one; two in the chest and one in the gut. He slumped down to his side and found he had a perfect view of the Vic's bedroom entrance. The boy fought for his life against four professionals. He was a goner. They bloodied him up pretty good before he finally collapsed on the floor. They picked him up like a piece of meat and placed him inside a cloth sack. One man threw it over his shoulder, headed to where there used to be a window, and tossed it out.

"Let's go," the man said, snapping his fingers.

The enforcer felt himself being picked up and given the same treatment. As he landed on a cushion below, his wound seared and everything went black. He tried to force his eyes to see, to no avail. Someone dragged him off the cushion and placed him on a hard surface. He heard a door slam.

"Stick him." a man ordered.

"He's out. I put three in him."

"Just in case. He's a tough fucker."

He felt the pinprick of a needle and cursed his body for not being able to move earlier. Before his consciousness fell into oblivion, he came to one conclusion.

*These guys were not from a rival family.*

⌒

General Perrara knocked on Hana's office door and found him perusing a digital map on the desk. He looked up and smiled at him.

"How's it looking so far?"

"We have incoming on a daily rotation," Hana replied.

"Really?"

Hana's face scrunched up.

"Some of them are bad." His expression saddened.

"Yes, some still treat Bi-Genetics like garbage."

"Or worse."

"Well, this is just one part of the program. I am going to send out some people for the bigger fish."

"Are you certain, this is the right thing to do?"

He saw Hana's resolve waiver for a moment, which was understandable. He had seen images of what state Hana was in when professor Makoto took him out of the Japanese facility.

"It gets better, I promise. We're not putting them through hell for the fun of it. Not like that."

"That I know," Hana said. "I meant the program itself. We do all this and still lose. And then we might have to deal with new monsters."

He glanced upwards and Perrara realized he meant the alien trainers. True, there was a certain vibe they gave off that made him feel uneasy.

"If it goes south," Perrara started his pitched.

Hana raised a hand to stop him.

"Not even Darnizva can help us."

⌒

Chow halls usually didn't fill with excess noise. A soldier got in, got chow, and got out. No time for chatter. The line moved along like a well-oiled machine. Today was an exception because a fight broke out between two fresh officers.

From his vantage point a couple of tables down, the observer continued to eat while watching the mess unfold. He could barely hear what they were shouting at each other. Phrases like 'pampered' and 'overrated' were aimed at his target who grabbed the other soldier by the balls while in a headlock. The other soldier howled in pain, his knees buckling, and his target sent him flying with a full-frontal knee in the face.

The MPs came busting in and hauled off both men, literally dragging them out of the hall. Everyone else resumed eating. The show was over. Finishing his meal, the observer stood with tray in hand and went to the bussing area. That done, he walked out whistling, adjusting his cap. As the adjunct for the military police, the two soldiers would be assigned to him for disciplinary action. The jackass who started it he would throw in the brig for a while. His target; he had another plan for.

Inside his office, he sat twirling in his chair, not looking at the young soldier who stood at ease before him.

"Ensign Damon Peters, reporting as ordered." He gave a curt salute.

"Sit down, soldier."

"Sir, yes sir!" He relaxed and took the seat across from him.

"Tell me," the observer began, "how you have gotten into three fights in the course of a year?"

"Not sure, sir. I don't start these things."

"No." The observer stopped twirling and sat correctly at his desk. "But you didn't need to engage either. If you get any more marks on your records, we may have to let you go."

Peterson's expression went grim. He had joined for two reasons. One was to get away from his privileged status even though he grew up in an orphanage, and two, to prove something to himself, along with everyone else. The observer had watched him struggle through basic training, then A school. This was not the first time they had a heart to heart talk.

"Sir, am I not allowed to defend my honor and my person?"

"Son," the observer sighed heavily, "No one is saying that. You have to pick your battles."

Peterson nodded in agreement. His short haircut was getting a bit long in the bangs and a few strands of hair fell in front of his eyes. Brushing them away, he sat up straighter.

"I understand, sir. I'll remember that."

"I'm reassigning you."

"What?" Peterson's eyes went wide and his face contorted into anger.

The observer gave him a look that changed that. Realizing how he had responded, Ensign Peterson went rigid with fear.

"I'm sorry, sir. I didn't mean to…"

The observer raised a hand to stop him.

"That is one of the reasons, right there. No need to pack your stuff, it's already being sent ahead." Shocked, Damon leaned back in the chair. "I think you would be better off letting off steam in an environment where you need to mind your P's and Q's."

Anger rose up in Peterson again, this time with teeth clenched, holding in whatever he wanted to say. Those dark blue eyes had a storm brewing in them. He may not have been the one who started the fights, but he was usually the first one to throw a punch.

"You leave at zero seven hundred."

"That's in forty-five minutes!" He drew back. "Sir."

"Sure is. Better double time it. Dismissed."

Ensign Peterson shot up from the chair, face pink,

and saluted. Then he pivoted to the door and let himself out.

The observer smirked as he rocked in his seat. Sitting up, he pulled open the bottom drawer and took out his wrist commlink.

*Another one in the bag.*

⌒

High-ranking officials lounged around in the hotel ballroom before the private dinner began. Every year, those involved with the alien business gathered to make sure everyone stayed on the same page. Rules were in place to ensure a safe haven and no one involved would be denied. General Hoskins found that hilarious as he strolled in with authority. His son, Chad, walked alongside him.

He still considered him a boy, even at nearly thirty years old. Already a colonel, his son had adopted his agenda, now heading up a Terror unit of his own. He, too, despised how the alien race that infiltrated their planet, albeit a crash, had asserted themselves. An almost spitting image of when the general was his age.

*That's just good fucking genes, there.*

Off to his left, he saw General Perrara having a drink with his wife. The son was a few feet away, surrounded by giggling women. A priss and a pervert, like his father in his book. Perrara caught sight of him as he turned to look around. He smiled and raised his glass. Hoskins hissed, then put on a winning smile.

"Come on, junior. Let's go say hello," he said through his teeth.

"I'm not junior! And why should we have to suck up to that bastard?"

"Because, it's what we need to do," Hoskins was getting irritated. "Bring your ass on."

Reluctantly, his son followed.

"Colonel Hoskins, how good to see you," General Perrara greeted him.

"General, sir."

"No need for the formalities tonight, son."

"I'm not your son."

Hoskins elbowed him in the ribs and watched his son barely wince, taking in the pain.

"Sorry, I'm a little uneasy here."

Perrara smiled and his wife beamed at him in that sickening lovey dovey way.

"Hoskins, don't chastise the young man too much." He gave a wink.

"It's General Hoskins. Or have you forgotten?"

"Not at all," Perrara replied. "As I've said. This is a laid-back kind of gig."

"You need to respect my father," his son said. "I gave you the courtesy as you did me, so you should keep up that example."

Mrs. Perrara's face blanched and Perrara halted his glass mid sip. A few of the guests turned towards them with looks of awe. Hoskins put on a perma-grin and tried not to look too obvious. He always told the boy to watch his tongue around these things. There was no putting a leash on that dog. A presence appeared behind him and out of the corner of his eye, he saw the younger Perrara.

"Now, see." Rubio, Perrara's son said. "I thought he was being very cordial. Those two have known each other about as long as we've been alive, and calling each other by title is nothing to get bent out of shape about." He turned to Hoskins and did the same wink as his father. "Isn't that right, General?"

Hoskins burst out laughing. Tears formed in his eyes. Catching his breath, he nodded and joined in the game.

"Whew! Perrara, you got some kid here."

"Oh, I do know." Perrara continued sipping his drink.

Hoskins gave his son a love tap in the ribs.

"You got something you need to say?"

His son's face turned pink and his eyes burned with indignation.

"Again, my apologies. Excuse me."

He turned and headed for the bar. The younger Perrara's gaze tracked him the whole way.

*What the hell is that about?*

"Mother, let's dance." Young Rubio took the champagne glass out of her hand and whisked her away to the dance floor. "Let's show them something good."

Alone together, Hoskins and Perrara stared each other down. This being a safe haven, neither one could do much to the other. Hoskins' lip twitched.

"So, what are you up to these days, Perrara?" He said the man's name like spit.

"Oh, that's none of your concern." Perrara frowned.

"Hmm. Heard one of our old contractor warehouses went up in a barbeque. Just hoping you ain't doing nothing shady." Hoskins gave a playful look.

Perrara surprised him by setting his glass down and coming so close they exchanged breathing air. Hoskins leaned away a bit.

"If you ever compromise my work again, I'll end you."

"What are you talking about?" Hoskins asked sweetly.

"And there will be no one to help you, not even your own son."

Perrara stepped back and retrieved his drink.

"Excuse me. I need a refill at the bar." He stopped halfway across the room. "You should take advantage of the bar, Hoskins. No telling when we might have a chance for another one of these things."

Hoskins clenched his fists and turned to see his

diminishing backside.

*Just you wait. I'll have my day.*


After giving his mother a few turns on the dance floor, Rubio released her to go to the powder room. He met his father at the bar and leaned on the wood platform.

"So," he said. "I think we should really find a way to get rid of him sooner than later."

His father glanced sideways at him. That look was a warning.

"I'm just saying."

"Even if we did, his son would take up the reins."

"We can't handle him?"

His father sighed and stood up straight.

"In my opinion, that boy is far more dangerous. We need to keep him contained."

"Boy? You sound like General Hoskins." That angered his father a bit.

"I am not amused."

"Lighten up, dad. We have time. Plus, his father is going to slip up."

"Let's hope so."

He stared into his father's eyes.

"I meant, he's going to get himself killed."

"Son," Perrara said.

"What he did at that warehouse."

"I know!" He slammed his drink on the bar and a man not far away jumped. "Sorry," he said to the man who walked away.

"We can't have incidents like that knowing he did them and not have him pay the consequences."

"Leave it be. I have plans for him."

Rubio raised his eyebrows, intrigued.

There was something sinister in his father's face, and

he kind of liked it. Then again, Hoskins deserved whatever was coming to him.

◠

The silver-eyed preteen, Eldan, walked up the driveway of his home in a cheerful mood. He had aced all of his quizzes and got to beat up the boy who tried to take his media player during study period. Of course, he had help from the Marzonetti kid. All that mattered was the end result. He let himself in and dropped his backpack on the sofa. His mother hated that because the thing was cream colored. It made him laugh every time, because she got so upset over something so trivial.

*Buy a different couch.*

In the kitchen, he grabbed a bottle of juice out of the refrigerator and gulped down the contents. He set the empty bottle on the counter and left. That's what the maid was for. He passed her on the way out, and she frowned at him.

"May Fong! Please go to the store and pick up some supplies."

His mother's voice rang out and the maid stopped dead in her tracks. She turned towards the sound of his mother coming down the stairs. She had a piece of paper in her hand.

"I've made a list for you." She came up to the maid and placed it in her palm.

"Of course, my lady, as soon as…"

"You will go now."

His mother's gaze dripped with fury.

"Yes, ma'am."

The maid hurried to the front door, grabbed her coat, and left. His mother didn't move until she heard the maid's car drive off. Then she turned on him.

Her hand wrapped around his neck, lifting him

off the floor until they were eye to eye. His struggle to release her grip was like trying to pry apart iron bars.

*Why?*

"You filthy mongrel. I should have drowned you when you were a baby. I should have known."

His father came down the stairs carrying a wooden cane. It was from when he had a skiing accident years ago and he kept it for nostalgia. There was no reason for him to have it in his hands now.

Eldan became frightened.

"The only reason we tolerate you in our midst is because we hadn't seen any indication you would shift or come connected in some foul way with another boy," his father said. "Obviously, we were wrong."

"Do you like sneaking around with your little boy-friend?" his mother seethed.

"I." he couldn't get much else out because she started to shake him.

His legs swayed and deciding to fight, swung his feet as hard as he could, striking her in the hip. It was in the nick of time because his father had come close, bringing the cane at him as if he were a piñata. His mother cried out in pain, dropping him, as his father missed and stumbled forward, tripping over his mother. He made a break for it and ran out of the house.

Their property on the east side expanded up to the edge of a river. On the other side of that was a freeway. He figured if he got there, he could wave someone down and get some help. He didn't understand why his parents were trying to harm him and he wasn't going to stick around to find out.

*Boyfriend?*

He thought about that for a minute and winced. The Marzonetti kid. He was always trying to be affectionate with him, kissing him on more than one occasion.

*But that didn't add up to this. Unless.*

His parents despised Bi-Genetics. He knew from the last physical he had when the doctor told them he was one. They never said anything though.

While he ran, not paying attention to how far his parents were behind him, pain struck him right in the shin, surprising him. He went toppling onto the wet grass. His mother grabbed him by the hair and dragged him up. Her fist caught the side of his head and he saw stars. The cane hit him on the tailbone and he blacked out for a split second.

Rage overcame him as it subsided, and he twisted himself out of his mother's grip. He was twelve, not helpless. He attacked his mother first, hitting her repeatedly in the ribs while using her as a shield from the cane blows his father delivered. With all his might, he pushed and sent them both to the ground together. He turned back towards the direction of the river and continued to run, thinking he had a good head start. The pain in his head and back screamed at him. He pushed on, determined to make his destination.

The river came into view and he forced himself forward. Not fifty yards from it, he heard what sounded like a banshee and his blood ran cold. His mother knocked him in the back of the head and he went down. That gave them the perfect opportunity, and they took it. Fists and cane rained down on him in quick succession for what seemed like an eternity. His vision blurred, and his body went slack, no longer able to fight.

It began raining and after some time, his parents stopped. Breathing hard, they stood back and looked around. He could taste his own blood.

*What are you waiting for?* He screamed at them silently. *Get it over with!*

His father finally moved towards him. Lifting him

up by the underarms, he dragged Eldan to the river. There, he tossed him in and walked away. Rejoining his mother, the two headed back to the house that lay so far away.

*Wait! Don't leave me!*

The tears felt like needles in his eyes and he felt coldness fill his whole body. He had heard enough about dying to know this was probably that feeling. He was dying and for what? Anger hit him, lasting only a bit before sadness and regret. At twelve years old, he had done absolutely nothing in life. His eyes closed as the pain went away.

Two men in a two-door car pulled up to the guard-rail along the freeway. The passenger got out with a pair of binoculars and aimed them at the river below.

"Got him."

"How does he look?" The driver asked as he came around to stand next to him.

"Not good. They did a number on him."

"Let's get him out of there."

The driver popped the trunk and took out a water-proof body bag made from breathable tarp material. Leaving the trunk open, the two men climbed over the rail and went down to the river. Every step, slippery due to the rain making the grass slick and the dirt below into mud.

They reached Eldan, and the passenger knelt beside him for a quick assessment.

"A lot of broken bones. He's out cold."

"Not dead?"

"No, but barely alive."

Positioning the bag right up on him, they slowly, gently scooped him into it and closed it up.

Instead of trying to lift him and do anymore damage,

they dragged the bag up. The slick grass created a slip and slide. At the railing, they both nodded and together picked him up. They stepped over the rail and maneuvered to the trunk. In went the boy's limp body. Slamming it shut, they got in the front seat and the driver took them out onto the road. The rain came down harder.

As head observers, the two spies watched from their observation room inside the bunker. They too went into the field occasionally, in addition to their main duty. Both veterans of espionage and being ghosts, their new gig kept them in high spirits. They still did their regular job for their government and found it boring compared to being part of the Shadow Organization. The Russian snorted as he thought of the name. Being a ghost meant invisibility, something other worldly. Shadows were much more frightening. Close to you, seen yet unseen. A silhouette attached to every single person.

His female counterpart, the female Italian, sat next to him with headphones on listening to the footage playing on the holoscreen in front of her. She had a grim look on her face. He glanced over at it and sighed. Every extraction, (because kidnapping sounded too sinister,) reminded him of humanity's decline since the revelation of hybrid humans. She whipped the headphones off and tossed them on the control panel.

"Not to your liking," he asked

"What do we say? Get in and out. Do not engage."

"Unless necessary."

She gave him a look of disapproval. He shrugged.

"They should have just dropped the parents, snatched the boy and left."

The Russian laughed, imagining the scene going down in such a prominent neighborhood. Efficient, yes, but it would raise too many questions. At least this way there was some rhyme or reason to it.

"At least we got him. They can triage him enroute."

"We had a few of those scenarios. I don't like it."

"Of course not. We're talking about children."

"And the military personnel we've acquired? What about them?"

He sat farther back in his chair and folded his arms. Aliens were coming to destroy the human race and what do we do? Keep fighting amongst ourselves, apparently. Countries still waged war on each other despite having a world military and government council. Conflict was still a concern and nowhere near the levels like before.

"We'll just have to endure until everything is in place."

"Think we can hold out another ten, twenty years? We're not getting any younger."

"Even if I have to resort to having alien DNA injected, I am staying for the long haul."

She reached down and pulled out a bottle of whiskey. Holding it up, she swung it back and forth. The smile on her face spoke volumes. He got the glasses out of the drawer on his side and did the same with them. They laughed as she poured a hefty amount in each glass. Raising the glasses high, they toasted each other.

"Prost!"

"Salud!"

Telia stood naked at the window of her quarters and gazed at the forest below. Its density made it perfect for ambushes. Earth was not as bad as she had imagined based on her intel. Many flaws were to be expected with a race not yet quite advanced enough for long range space travel. A small blip sound made her avert her stare from the scenery.

Along the far end of her room sat a commlink synced with a holoscreen that came to life. A message flashed on it intermittently. She read the words, written in English, and smiled.

SEVENTY-TWO PERCENT COMPLETION RATE

The time was almost upon her and the aliens who came with her to begin training the fragile humans. After being informed that they were actually hybrids, she still had no faith in their strength. These were beings not raised to their full potential. In fact, their governments restrained them from using any inherent talents unless it served warmongering.

War.

She turned back to her view and frowned. Many of the races she knew of didn't try to annihilate each other. Their enemy was another race. Civilizations similar to Earth perished because of it. When you diminish your own fighters, another race can swoop in and take over or destroy. That is how she saw Earth at the moment.

A stirring on the bed broke her thoughts. She turned her head towards it and saw her mate rolling over. He clutched the pillow close to his face and nearly curled up in a fetal position. She grinned. So young and beautiful. He was one of many she had in her circle and never spent too much time with. He was loyal to a fault. Since this trip was short, she figured it would be enough to mold him into the ideal mate. Young he may be, but also one of the deadliest warriors she had seen in over a century.

"Wake up, my sweet warrior. Time to prepare for incoming."

He stirred again, this time stretching his whole body. The covers pushed away as he did this exposed the naked upper half of him. She smiled, seeing his muscular body toned in all the right places.

"All the sacrificial lambs are gathered?" He asked. His voice sounded a bit rough.

"Almost." She nodded towards the holoscreen.

He sat up, letting his vision adjust. A grimace followed.

"Let me know when it's one hundred."

He rolled over on his side, presenting his backside to her. She walked over and climbed atop him, grabbing his ass hard. She leaned close and whispered in his ear.

"I gave you a direct order, my sweet. Should I tear you limb from limb to prove a point, or do you obey me?"

His eyes flew open as he turned his head. Their noses touched and she could see every spec in his irises. And the fear.

"My apologies. I was only joking. Of course, I'll obey."

She let go of her grip and gave a hard pat instead.

"Good." She kissed him. "Let's take one of those warm showers, hmm?"

As they got up together, she lingered behind a bit and stared at the message again. Feeling more energized than before, she tapped the acknowledgement icon on the screen and followed her mate into the bathroom.

## HIERARCHY

The bunker buzzed with life as soldiers prepared to add the finishing touches to the obstacle course. The first ones to go through would be current military personnel from the master list of soldiers with modified DNA, not Bi-Genetics. As for their part in the agenda, they were close to the bottom tier.

Hana looked over the program details again while chaos went on outside his office. With so many levels within, he almost couldn't keep it all straight. Persons of interest were assigned based on the master list. From public servants to an elite group, each tier was special. Starting from the bottom was ideal to see how it would go moving forward.

The other reason was the children assigned to the elite group were still being prepped. Not necessarily repaired though, well enough to move on their own. He had seen some of them and felt sick thinking about it. His parents had tossed him away as a baby, so he was raised in the facility. As awful as the place was, at least he knew what to expect. These kids thought they had parents who cared enough to keep them for as long as they did.

A soldier came and knocked on the doorframe. Hana looked up to address him. The name on his tag said Sgt. Scott Mitchum.

"What do you need, sergeant?"

"Incoming," was all he said.

Hana stood up and grabbed his tablet.

"Let's go."

The two hurried down the corridors through three levels before ending at the bunker entrance on the far side. From the platform above the second hangar, he could see the truckloads of soldiers coming in. There were six in all, carrying about twenty each. The soldiers had been told that the completion of the obstacle course would determine their assignments and fate in the armed forces.

Even with altered DNA, some of them still didn't have much control over their new abilities. This would force them to at least try. One out of every eight were not altered soldiers because the General wanted to see if a normal human could do it just as well. He would always say not to underestimate mankind. The soldiers exited the trucks and lined up single file per their training. Hana chewed his bottom lip as he took stock of them.

"What do you think, as someone who made it through that abomination called a course?"

Sergeant Mitchum leaned over the platform's railing and looked closer. After a while, he stood up.

"I'd say maybe a third will make it."

"That's all?" His assessment shocked Hana.

"The cocky ones are going to be in for a rude awakening. The ones not prepared will get hurt. That leaves the ones with no preconceived notions of what they're going to encounter."

"I think I should keep you around a lot longer."

"Glad to be of service."

They made their way down to greet the soldiers and lead them to the queue stations.

The command center for the obstacle course sat above level with windows that overlooked the entire habitat. Holoscreen monitors were up and running along the panels. A full crew of technicians set up their stations. Each soldier would go in a staggered order so as not to bunch up. If a soldier lagged too far behind, the next in line would have to wait.

"Ready to commence operations," the head of the course yelled out.

Hana heard it loud and clear through the earpiece he had and nodded to Sergeant Mitchum who stepped forward in front of the large group.

"Listen up! You're going to follow me into the holding pen and five of you will go into standby stations. In the stations, you will have time to settle your nerves and pick out supplies. Any weapons you may need are also available." A hand raised. "No questions! Good luck!"

He pivoted to the sliding door that Hana used a keycard to open and led them in. They all plopped their gear down and sat on the white benches scattered throughout the all-white room. Some soldiers winced at the brightness. Another soldier came around with a sack and shook it up each time a soldier reached in to pull out a number tag. When the sack was empty, Sergeant Mitchum cleared his throat.

"One through five, follow me."

The soldiers picked up their gear and complied. At a narrow corridor were five black doors with digital numbers one through five on each one. They didn't have to be told to go in. When the last one was secured inside, Hana and Mitchum left the area to wait in the command center.

The monitor on the upper right showed each soldier in their standby stations. The technician in front of it pushed a commlink and spoke.

"In the bin you will find an earpiece and goggles. These will communicate to us everything you see and hear inside the environment." He waited until each candidate grabbed one and fitted them on their person. "You will have fifteen minutes to gear up with either personal equipment or the ones provided in the hidden cabinets behind you."

All the soldiers pushed the wall panels and watched an arsenal appear. Some of them whistled at the impressive display. General Perrara pulled no punches when it came to weapons.

"At the fifteen-minute mark, a buzzer will sound and a door will appear on your right. Once you pass this door, it will disappear and there will be no turning back. You have three hours to finish the course."

"Three hours!" One soldier exclaimed. "What the hell kind of course is this?"

"What the fuck's in there?" Another asked.

The first soldier merely paused at the time frame, then resumed gearing up. The third paid it no mind, and the fourth sat down to contemplate something before getting back to attach his sidearms.

"My heart is pounding," Hana said. He had a hand on his chest, gripping his shirt.

"This is exciting," the technician said. He turned to his associate on the other end. "Get medical ready."

"Already done."

To the commlink, the technician spoke again.

"This course will test your reflexes, observation skills, decision making, and marksmanship. Good luck, soldiers."

The buzzer went off, and the first group of soldiers went through the door.

At the three-hour mark, only one soldier came out the other end of the course. Battered and completely exhausted, he made it past the threshold and fell face down on the white-tiled floor. Medical personnel rushed towards him and got him onto a stretcher. In the command center, technicians were ready to make the call on two soldiers who appeared to not be moving inside the middle part of the course. The other two were still trying to make it through. Because of the ones not moving, the fourth group of five were on a delay.

Sergeant Mitchum gripped the edge of the console in the command center and shook his head. From the looks of the one who made it on time, the course had pushed his body more than it could handle. On the holoscreen, he saw movement. A downed candidate tried getting up. By the way he moved, the soldier was in no shape to finish.

"Call it," he ordered.

The technician next to him pushed the commlink.

"Medical staff needed in level four of the obstacle course. Two down."

In the holding pen and the standby stations, the soldiers looked up at the speakers in the rooms. Looks of horror and panic across the board. Some of them began pacing, others became nervous.

Seeing this, Mitchum tsked.

If that was enough to scare them, then all was lost. If another soldier made it, they would come out in the next twenty minutes. The timer floating above them counted down. Every three hours it would reset.

Each group had its own timer. With only one person through so far, the results looked daunting. At the six-minute mark, before the next reset, another soldier came through. Two more came not far afterwards.

That made four from the first two groups to complete

the course. They came more frequently as the day went on, just not the way Hana thought. Medical was working hard to get the soldiers treated in a timely fashion before the next round showed up. In a sense, the first test of the obstacle course counted as a failure.

"Well, that was entertaining," Telia said.

The four aliens were in their command center in the lower level of the bunker, watching the feed from the obstacle course. They sat in large papasan like chairs that floated high above the floor. Below, technicians were testing equipment. None of them looked up at the aliens out of fear.

Karias sat with one arm resting on his knee, chin in hand. His expression was one of disgust. It signaled him having no patience for such weak resolve in the humans. Lindo just sat back in a stupor at the soldiers' level of failure.

"What a waste of alien DNA. All that and they couldn't manage this?"

Attar plucked a piece of fruit from his lap and tossed it into his mouth. He seemed to have an affinity for them lately. She concurred with Lindo on this matter. Their underwhelming performance dashed her high hopes of seeing an altered human in action.

"Maybe it's because of their age," Lindo said. "We may have better luck with the children."

She tapped her lower lip.

"Yes, that's probably the case." A devious smile formed. "I look forward to molding them into great warriors."

That smile carried on to the other three and they sat with those expressions, scaring the workers more than they already were.

All the top officials within the Shadow Organization assembled in the main conference room of an undisclosed office building. General Perrara greeted them before the meeting started. His son helped with the seating arrangements. This was going to be a formal breakdown of how the organization would operate as it pertained to the training groups. It would also be the first time seeing each other.

In the beginning, Perrara felt secrecy was the key, realizing quickly it only worked for the observers and their operatives. Not knowing the chain of command meant toes would get stepped on. He nipped that in the bud quickly. A presentation queued up on the main screen.

With everyone seated, he cleared his throat to signal attention.

"Good afternoon, ladies and gentlemen. As you know, he had a few incidents where assignments crossed each other. I figured this would be a good time for all of us to get acquainted, so we can know who is in play going forward."

He stepped to the podium on the edge of the platform and used the remote clicker to start the presentation. The organization's logo displayed.

"I also want to go over the different sections within the organization. Each tier is crucial, depending on the situation. Starting from the bottom, here are the first two." He clicked to the next slide that showed the bottom section of a graph. "Law enforcement. We are recruiting a certain number to assist with any investigations that we may need help on. The second is standard military personnel. If there is a minor job to be done, they are the ones to do it."

One of the military men raised a hand.

"When you say job?"

"Open for interpretation," Perrara answered.

"Infiltrations? Assassinations? What are we talking?"

"No. That is for the next two tiers. I mean routine."

"Oh. Sorry to interrupt you, then. Please continue."

Perrara clicked to show more of the pyramid graph.

"Next up is our military elite. They will do infiltrations into other countries if necessary. Secret operations that not even the main branches get to know about."

"Fair enough," another high ranked military person said. "Whatever it takes to keep it off the books is game for me."

"Then we have our usual network of spies and ghosts." Everyone nodded. "There was no reason to keep them out of the loop. They are actually working as observers and operatives. Their identities are secret from all of us for good reason. That is why we can only communicate via code. They conduct their own meetings when it is deemed viable to do so."

"I don't like it. They could be up to anything and your fear of stepping on each other's toes pertains to them as well."

"Rest assured, they know how the game is to be played." He moved on to another slide. "Trainers. As you know, we have human and alien ones. The aliens will train the humans, who will then train our candidates. On occasion, the aliens will also engage with candidates during the advanced stages."

"That I really don't like," the first military person from before said. "They seem to have an ulterior motive for doing this on our behalf."

"Noted. I am inclined to feel the same, but it's too late for that now." Perrara clicked the remote again and only the top of the pyramid was visible. "The final piece of the puzzle."

The screen only had one name: SHADOWMEN.

"The goal is for our candidates to become the most elite fighters. Our fame and glory called Shadowmen. More than ghosts or special forces military. A fearsome group of individuals that know no rivals."

Loud hisses and outcries erupted around the room. So many questions and insults were thrown at him all at once.

"And who will control these monsters?"

"Have you gone mad? We can't unleash something like that!"

"What in God's name are you thinking?"

He stood and waited for it to die down. When everyone was calm, red faced with anger, he answered them.

"The same way we control our soldiers. Or do you feel we aren't doing that efficiently?"

He gave them a smile that conveyed his disdain. Some in the room became visibly pale. To imply that they had no handle on their troops was like a slap in the face and pushing it their own fault.

"Okay, fine," a government agent said. "It still remains we are essentially creating monsters. Let's not sugarcoat this."

Perrara leaned on the podium and let the group talk amongst themselves.

*I know all too well.*

Professor Makoto deemed swordsmanship training mandatory. He explained it as bringing back some sense of honor in fighting. Telia studied footage and indeed found it fascinating. She understood what he meant since sword fighting required one-on-one combat. A test of strength and will to determine who would be victorious.

In the combat room, she held a katana. One of many supplied by the Asian government. She tested its weight, swing diameter and blade span. The weapon felt quite light and deadly. Especially on her hands. She noticed because with her skills and the amount of force she produced, the blade could cut through most solid objects. Of course, a few of the swords snapped from her trials.

Off on the other side of the room were her counterparts, also testing their swings. Today, they would battle to see how long the new blades they had developed would last. The humans would get regular ones until they were more advanced.

"Are we ready, my comrades?" She asked them.

The three males turned to her in unison with menacing looks.

*Good.*

She positioned herself into a stance and gave them her most winning smile.

"Come."

And they did. She blocked all three and stopped them in their tracks before pushing them back. The two Chombrazens split apart and came at her from either side, while her mate ran up the side of the wall and leaped down towards her. She smirked. With lightning speed, she engaged all of their swords, creating an impenetrable field of air around her. Movement towards the lower section caught her eye just in time and she bent backwards as a sword swiped across her body.

Not letting them get a chance to follow through, she catapulted herself out of the fray and landed on the other side of the room. She laughed.

"So much fun. I like these toys!"

The three males stood straight, swords extended and waited for her to finish laughing. When she cocked her head to one side, taunting them, they advanced on her again. This time, she turned her back on them and let them get closer. The grin on her face as she turned to engage them was downright frightening.

Hana had been curious about what the aliens were up to the past few months. He went into the command center and watched the feed from the combat room with hands clamped down on the console's edge. His knuckles were white from the strain and a headache formed from gritting his teeth for so long.

"That could kill a human instantly," Mitchum said.

Hana jumped and clutched his shirt. His eyes wide, he cursed himself for displaying such a reaction.

"Sorry," Mitchum said. "I didn't mean to scare you."

"No, it's fine." He let go of his shirt and took a few deep breaths. "I was a bit too engrossed in watching."

"Yeah, but I stand by what I said."

They turned back to the screen, flinching when Telia struck the big Chombrazen with such force the alien hit the wall with a loud thud, like a bulldozer going through concrete.

"Still think this program is a good idea?" Mitchum asked.

"It's too late now. We go forward and hope we don't have to use those regeneration chambers they brought."

"Oh, we'll be using them," Mitchum said. "A lot."

Storm clouds gathered above in the desert sky and the group waiting at the main gate of the bunker looked up as one. Once again, Hana came out to greet more incoming, his tablet held tight in his hands. He felt sorry for them knowing what was in store. The guards instructed them forward. He marked them off one by one as another soldier scanned their wristbands' barcode. Inside the bunker, he led them to the aliens' command center.

The large doors opened and the first thing they all saw were the floating platforms, each holding an alien.

The group stopped at the entrance, not wanting to move any further. Guards positioned in the rear had to push them in. Hana found it unnerving as well that the group consisted of well-trained assassins from around the world.

"Ahh, our first lambs have arrived," Telia cooed.

"Trash," Karias said.

"Can we just get it over with and kill them all now?" Attar asked.

Lindo remained silent.

His expression conveyed a consensus.

Some of the group members took offense by clenching fists and teeth. That only made Telia laugh. In the blink of an eye, she had one man in her grip and brought him face to face.

"Are you angry, human?" Her eyes glowed as her mouth spread wide to reveal teeth.

He grabbed her wrist to try prying her fingers off his neck. When that didn't work, he used his other hand to hit her in the chin with the bottom of his palm. She didn't flinch from the blow as her smile widened. With ease, she took hold of his arm, and wrenching it backward, pulled. The sound of a wet sponge being rung along with sharp pops were accompanied by the man screaming. Blood rained down onto the floor.

When a few soldiers moved to help him, Hana shook his head in horror. The man's eyes glazed over and he stopped screaming as his arm dangled from his body. His eyes remained locked on the female alien, and she seemed pleased.

"Take him to the chamber. I like this one." She dropped him like a sack of garbage and sailed back up to her cushioned platform above.

As a medical tech came rushing in to tend to the man, Hana gulped and stepped closer.

"That was unnecessary," he managed to get out.

"Of course it was," Telia replied. "They need to know we are not here to baby them. Training means death. If they can survive that, then they can train the rest of your pitiful race."

Hana frowned, gripping his tablet close to his chest. "I just…"

"Is that not the goal?" Karias snapped.

A few in the shaken group wiped their mouths after vomiting. Among them, many had seen such atrocities. For some reason, this hit differently. The ones who had steel resolve were contemplating their situation. For the first time, Hana feared some of them may decide to back out of the program. If that happened, they wouldn't be allowed to leave. Not alive, anyway.

"Training sessions will start in one week. I hope you are prepared to face oblivion."

Telia stared down at them.

"I brought them here for an introduction," Hana said, angered.

"I gave them one."

Hana turned to the guards.

"Let's go."

With the group being ushered out, the three male aliens looked over at Telia accusatory. She turned her head and stared at them with indignation. Finally, she spoke.

"Hana, my sweet." Hana gave her a woeful look. "I am sorry. That's not what you meant, was it? I will do a proper introduction at the training session, I promise."

"Fine." Hana's heart was breaking.

Inside his office, Hana dropped to his knees, shaking and cried. He yelled at the floor and pounded it with his fists. He had never wanted to see such cruelty and carnage ever again. Flashbacks from his time in the facility bent him over until his forehead touched the floor. The tears wouldn't stop.

Arms folded around him and pulled him close. He couldn't see them because his vision had gone blurry, and he didn't care either. Just having someone near was enough. He buried his head in the uniform shirt of a soldier and continued to cry.

Telia brought up her own holoscreen and watched Hana's breakdown. Her face scrunched up. Something about seeing the little man-child in pain made her feel ill. Being intrusive, she tapped into Hana's mind and reared back in disgust. Her reaction perplexed the other three. She didn't tell them what she saw. Removing the screen, her eyes burned with rage. It made her even more willing to break the candidates. Humans were indeed a disgusting species.

꙳

In the Oval Office, the President of the United States of America paced the floor while Darnizva sat stretched out on the sofa. He eyed the president carefully, not disturbing the man's obvious brooding. At some point, he finally stopped and looked over at Darnizva.

"I don't like being kept in the dark, Captain."

"What are you implying?"

"You said there was help coming to train our combined troops."

"That is correct."

"Yet, so far, many of the troops we were training have not been briefed. Where are the aliens that came to aid us?"

"I assure you, Mr. President, that they are indeed putting together a training doctrine."

"That's not what I mean," the president huffed.

"The troops you are referring to we tested and are not viable for the program. I have already arranged for the ones who are to be transferred to a facility of my choosing."

The President spun on him, his face nearly red.

"And that is the problem! Your choosing, not our joint leaders'!"

Darnizva swung his legs off the sofa to sit up straight. He stood up and approached the president, towering over the man. The president swallowed hard and leaned back a little from him.

"Yes, our fleet crash landed on this planet and you fail to realize that we are under no obligation to assist you. You asked for our help, and I have supplied it."

His face going pale, the president backed away.

"I'm sorry. It's just very frustrating when you have no answers for the rest of your allies."

"Who's asking questions?"

"Everyone." The president lifted his head higher. "You're not going to disclose the location of this facility, are you?"

"No."

The vice president came into the room with a similar look of defiance on his face and Darnizva watched the president give him some sort of private signal to nix it. The Vice President stopped in the middle of the room and turned to Darnizva.

"What's going on? Have we started preparations to move the troops into training?"

The president covered his face in exasperation.

"I'll explain later." He removed his hand and gave Darnizva a glare. "I still don't like it."

"You don't have a choice," Darnizva sat back down, "human."

The Vice president's head jerked up and he looked at

the President then Darnizva and back again. Realizing his tone sounded worse than he thought, Darnizva let out a sigh before speaking.

"That was uncalled for. But, you need to trust me." The President balked. "Unless, you don't want your civilization to survive."

All three stared at each other for a long time, those words like weights.

◦

Soldiers in states of over exhaustion, hypertension, and dehydration filled the bunker's medical wing to capacity. After the first round, those who completed the course were moved to a different sector. The ones who failed were given the option to retake the course in three months, being shipped back to their home bases. Those in medical came from the second round and it had nearly the same failure rate as the first.

General Perrara wondered if the course was maybe too tough, remembering only half the soldiers and his son had completed it in the allotted time. He didn't want to think of how weak the world's military truly was based on the results. When he came to check in on the progress, he found Hana looking worse for wear. The young assistant ran off the numbers as if in a muddled haze. It made him think there was some other reason.

Perrara strolled through the aisles, taking a glance at every soldier down for the count, many of them unconscious. One soldier had muscle spasms throughout his whole body. A sign of overexertion. The course pushed their bodies to maximum performance. A guard on the other side motioned for him and, curious, went to see what he wanted.

"Sir, I needed to tell you," the soldier whispered.

"About what?" he whispered back.

Not understanding why they were doing so.

"The female alien. She tore a man's arm right off in front of everyone."

Perrara reared back, his eyes narrowing into slits.

"When was this?"

"A week ago. You should have seen Hana's face."

The General stiffened.

*So that's it.*

He remained calm even though his fingers twitched, wanting to ball into fists.

"Why would she do such a thing?"

"To prove a point, I guess. They were the incoming trainers, and she made an example out of one."

"I get it, but why are we whispering," he finally asked.

The soldier came even closer to him and leaned towards his ear.

"Because they listen all the time."

Telia sat on her floating cushion in the command center and watched the two men whispering at each other inside her orb. She saw General Perrara look around above him for surveillance cameras and finding none. His demeanor changed to irritation, then he left the medical bay. She knew he would come straight to her.

Within half an hour, General Perrara came through the sliding doors of the command center. His purposeful stride had an air of caution. He at least knew who and what he was dealing with.

"General, how good of you to visit."

He looked around the room.

"You are alone?"

She smiled at him.

"For the moment, yes."

"I understand you had something akin to a small

demonstration last week."

Ahh.

"Of sorts."

He slumped forward and let out a sigh.

"That could have waited until the training started."

"Are you questioning my methods?"

She stared down at him and, although his eyes flinched, he didn't move from his spot.

*Such resolve,* she thought.

As he turned to leave, he called out, "Please try to restrain yourself. It scared Hana to death."

"Stay away from him," she replied. The General stopped. "The only ones he should fear are his own kind." He didn't turn back around. She could tell it shook him. "See you again soon, General."

Sun rays glistening across the river made it sparkle as if made of jewels. The gondola glided atop the water at a leisurely pace. People walked along the boardwalk enjoying the mild weather. Professor Morandi leaned back and savored the scented air. Across from her on the other side of the boat was her personal assistant. His long legs couldn't stretch out and appeared uncomfortable. He yawned.

"Kevin, were you listening to me?"

His head rested parallel to the sky with his eyes closed. The tight crewneck shirt and black slacks made him look like a supermodel. Professor Morandi averted her gaze. She could never stare at him for too long.

"What were we talking about?" His head rose as he opened his eyes.

*Beautiful.*

"I forbid you to go."

"It was bound to happen."

She wanted to find out Professor Makoto's agenda without sacrificing her prized champion. Kevin had pitched the the idea to insert himself in the scientist's circle to gain access to the secret location. It wouldn't be hard for him since General Perrara always had an interest in his talent. That was beside the point. She had let him go before when that other General and his unit stormed her facility, causing more damage than necessary.

"If they find out you are doing this for me and decide to silence you." She didn't finish.

He leaned over until his chin touched his knees, then cocked his head to one side.

"So, you think it would be that easy to do?"

Professor Morandi sat up.

"There's no telling what those two are involved in and it may be worse than we could ever have imagined."

"All the more reason."

He leaned back and resumed his lazy sprawl with his eyes closed.

She felt a sense of foreboding. Something sinister lurked on Earth, and smelled of doom.

Damon rode in the back of the transport truck along with nine other soldiers to some secret destination. Still raw with anger about being reassigned, he cursed his commanding officer. If he ever met the man again, a punch in the kidneys was in order.

Then he realized that way of thinking contributed to the main reasons he got shipped off. He rubbed at the wristband scribed with a barcode and his name. Tagged livestock. A quick glance around at the others, he concluded they were higher in rank and obviously had no interest in talking to each other.

*Fine by me.*

The truck rolled to a stop, and a soldier immediately whipped the flaps open to let in desert air. Damon coughed as the dry heat hit him. The sun had not yet dropped behind the horizon, its brightness burning with intense heat.

"Line 'em up!" the soldier outside ordered.

They all jumped down from the back of the truck and formed a single line at the entrance to a huge installation. It had hardly any windows and smacked of an updated prison. He had a thought that maybe his commanding officer did indeed send him to the brig, only far worse than the one on base.

Armed guards stood as sentry at the equally giant double doors that sat halfway opened, inviting them in.

"Proceed through and wait for instructions!"

As each soldier passed the first guard, he scanned their barcode and a blip sounded. Damon noticed the pretty boy holding a tablet inside the building. Definitely not military. Another soldier standing on his left scrutinized them as they came in.

His vision zeroed in on the name tag. He locked eyes with Sergeant Mitchum, and neither liked the other. Mitchum averted his gaze and bent his head down to whisper in the pretty boy's ear.

The double doors swung closed after letting in the last soldier. Its hydraulic system whirred, and a loud hiss emitted as the doors sealed shut. Ahead of them, the pretty boy made some announcement about an obstacle course and how it determined your rank and assignments. He barely listened out of spite. Whatever he meant to do here had no value to him. They had already cast him out of his unit.

The candidates were led into a white room where a man came with a sack. When it got to him, he pulled out a number tag. Sweet sixteen. Which meant he had some time on his hands to mentally get his shit together. He found an empty spot in the back and laid out, drifting off to sleep.

Nearly an hour passed before another soldier came to stand over him, blocking the light.

"Instead of taking a nap, how about you take this seriously?"

Damon opened his eyes and stared up at some meat head in fatigues.

"How about you mind your own business?"

"You see anyone else lounging around like it's a holiday?" The soldier's face scrunched up and became flushed. "There's no place for lazy bastards like you."

He swung his legs off the bench and sat up.

"Back off me."

"Or what?" The meat head's fist clenched.

"Step away from him," Sergeant Mitchum ordered. "Now!"

A buzzer blared, followed by numbers flashed up above on the wall. He was in the next group, along with the meat head. As they headed to their numbered doors, Damon made a quick maneuver with his arm and slammed the meat head into his door. He hit it hard with the sound of raw meat against metal. Blood trickled from his nose. The meat head roared, his rage intense, as he came at Damon.

Damon's door opened right as the meathead came in contact and he went in. As it shut, he snorted, then took notice of his surroundings, or lack of. The room was pure white. Tiny lines, barely visible, were indications of hidden panels.

This time, he listened to the instructions. Stripped of most of his own gear before departure, he opted for the logical choice of using the ones supplied. He whistled at the arsenal, then stepped back to get a good assessment.

All of those options meant they were necessary for whatever they encountered on the other side.

After a few minutes, he grabbed the night vision contact lenses, a bowie knife, two handguns, and an assault rifle. As an afterthought, he took the zipline wire. He wondered how many came and grabbed a shit ton of gear, or worse, not enough. Checking himself, he nodded in satisfaction at his choices.

Go with the essentials. Cuz, when you're out on a mission, that's all you got.

That's the one thing he learned from his shit turd commander.

*Man, I say shit a lot.*

The second buzzer sounded, and the hidden door revealed itself. He took a deep breath and stepped through. Darkness enveloped him before the contacts adjusted. A smile spread across his face.

*Easy Peasy.*


Sergeant Mitchum observed Damon from the moment he came into the bunker. It didn't surprise him when the soldier rammed the other into the door. In the command center, he noted every piece of gear he chose. After so many rounds of soldiers who went through the course, Ensign Peterson was the first to wear the night vision contacts. Others opted for the conventional goggle attachments.

He skimmed through Damon's file and saw a disciplinary record that any self-respecting delinquent would be proud of. The problem was, the military didn't take too kindly to that.

*Well, let's so how bad ass you really are.*

He checked the medical team on hand.

Two hours, seventeen minutes and twenty-two seconds displayed on the timer above the course exit doors and out came Damon. He stumbled forward, landing on his hands and knees. The first thing he ripped off was the flak jacket, then the mini video camera head band. He retched once.

Vomit spewed from his mouth and nose.

A medical crew person who came to help had her hand slapped away. When she tried again, he violently shoved her, and a fight ensued between him and the other two attendees as they tried to restrain him.

"Hold him!"

"What do you think I'm trying to do?" he yelled.

"Stick him already!"

"I did!" the attendee on the right seethed.

Distractiion left them vulnerable. Damon got loose, tossing all of them aside like rag dolls. Sergeant Mitchum came at him and before he could get too close, met him halfway, landing a punch. With his assailants down, Damon stood with ragged breathing, his mouth covered in vomit and drool. His vision was all fucked up, and he didn't want anyone to touch him. He clawed at his sweat soaked uniform and ripped the fabric to let in air.

"You motherfuckers!" He screamed with a rasp in his throat. "I'll kill you all!"

The room went Technicolor and tilted. A second wave of sickness came over him, his urge to throw up halted as he fell into a deep, dark pit.

When Ensign Peterson hit the floor like a brick, Mitchum stood up and went to check his pulse. A faint thumping from the vein against his fingers made him slump down, relieved. The medical crew got to work getting him onto a stretcher. They wheeled him out in a hurry.

He looked up at the timer and stared at it in disbelief. His personal best came just shy of the three-hour mark, the fastest; until now.

The course's grueling design pushed every part of the human senses and psyche. Peterson had probably snapped halfway through it, none the wiser. He had been watching on the monitors and saw no indication that the soldier was in danger psychologically.

Every tech in the command center waited for him to exit, the program now deemed a success by his completion score alone. Hana had already gone to his office to send out the report that included the stats.

Mitchum realized something went wrong by how Ensign Peterson approached the exit. Like a dying man reaching for light at the end of a tunnel. Staggering around as if he couldn't see. A madness had consumed him. That's why he ordered the medical staff to go in before him.

He never favored humans being injected with alien DNA for military purposes, and this solidified his thinking. Moving at such speeds defied human capabilities. Others in the program had used their new ability at great consequences. Broken bones, torn muscles, and ligaments were the price they paid.

I don't like this at all.

"I want that one," Telia announced.

She had also been watching from her command center and her mouth salivated as Damon moved through the course like a fiend. Her counterparts seemed interested as well. Down below, the program coordinator stood, waiting to give his report. The man's face paled at her request.

"He's slotted for military special forces detail."

Telia leaned forward.

Her eyes glowed as she bared her teeth.

"You will bring him into our fold," she hissed loudly.

The other three turned to him with fervent looks. He backed away.

"I will have to discuss this with General Perrara first," he stammered.

"No, you will not. You are the coordinator."

She sat back in her seat. A smile sweet as pie formed.

"If you do this, I would be forever grateful."

All the color drained from the coordinator's face. His eyes bulged out while his grip tightened on his tablet.

"He's in the medical bay being treated. In a week, perhaps?"

"Yes. One week." She clapped her hands together. "Now, tell me the progress report on my little darlings."

# THREE : RULES OF ENGAGEMENT

## TRAINING

Soft sobbing and sniffles emitted from inside the concrete holding cell. Twelve children, ranging from age twelve to fourteen, sat scattered about, scared, hungry, and cold. A tiny window twenty feet above let them know if it was day or night and they had been there for a few days already. The first couple of days were fraught with anger and yelling. As hunger and despair set in, the mood lessened. Some children were visibly hurt.

One in particular sat slumped against the back wall, staring into oblivion whenever he was awake and slept like the dead. His right arm was in a sling, bandages around both his ankles peeked from under the pants leg, and he wore an eye patch on his left eye. Small and pitiful. Another boy kept watch over him from across the way.

A slot opened at the bottom of the door.

"Time for chow," a voice spoke through it. "No stealing or negotiations. Everyone eats,"

One by one, small plates were pushed through. The kids who could move scrambled towards them and grabbed a plate, then headed back to their spots. Four of them remembered the others and fetched plates for them. Squeeze bottles of water came through as well.

The boy watching the wounded one set a plate in front of him and waited until the kid took hold of the cold cuts and shoved it in his mouth. He chewed slowly.

Satisfied that the kid could eat, the boy sat down next to him and did the same.

This went on for a few more days, with none of the children really speaking to one another. As many of them regained their strength, the fighting started again. Anxiety was high because they had no idea who their kidnappers were, or where they could be. One boy took to taunting the weaker ones, even attacking them when no one was looking.

Day ten saw the end to his reign.

This time, he went after the wounded kid.

"Hey cripple! Why don't you talk?"

He kicked him in the ankle. The boy's eyes went wide with pain and tears sprung up.

"What's wrong? Your parents throw you down the stairs? Or did you just get your ass kicked for being a pussy?"

He slapped the boy upside the head and laughed loudly. Then he stopped. The wounded boy let out a strangled animal sound and grabbed him by the arm. He began yanking him hard enough with good momentum that his body went crashing into the wall repeatedly. Blood splattered with each impact. When the mean kid fell to the floor after being released, the boy took his plate and hit him on the head until the kid's body was completely still.

Breathing hard, his face contorted with rage, the boy slumped back down in his usual spot and closed his eyes. His face softened before he fell asleep. The screaming of children backing away in terror didn't wake him. Only the boy who helped him most of the time didn't blink an eye at the scene.

For two days, the other boy's body lay on the floor, still holding on. A slight pulse felt whenever one of the other kids was brave enough to check. Finally, the doors opened, and two men came in to retrieve him. None of the children dared move or try to escape because there were two other armed guards at the door. As quickly as they came in was how they left. All that remained as a reminder was the dried blood splatter on the wall and floor.

The boy who helped the wounded kid kept his eyes on the door, not saying a word. A guard gave him a dirty look. None of the men wore masks which told plenty about their circumstance. If being seen didn't matter, then all of them were in deep trouble. He could only think of two scenarios where this was relevant. One, they were all going to die or two, their families knew who the kidnappers were.

He waited until the men left, sealing the door backup, and went to check on the wounded kid. Still asleep, his face showed signs of obvious pain. The way he went off the deep end when asked if his parents did that to him meant it was probably true.

*Man, he's a real cutie.*

At fourteen, he wasn't quite into the whole dating thing. He knew pretty when he saw it. Even in such a messed-up state, that reason is what drew him. Food came soon after and again, he gently shook the wounded boy awake so he could eat.

Loud booms followed by pieces of ceiling crack-ing and falling made the children rise in a panic. Some hugged the wall, frozen in fear, while others shielded themselves from the falling debris. The door splintered after the last boom and crumbled apart, leaving a gaping hole. In the distance, they could hear rapid gunfire. Dust and sand swirled into the room.

*It smells like a desert.*

The helper boy stood confused for a moment. None of the men appeared to be from a desert region and if indeed that's where they were, it was time to get the hell out. While children ran out of the room into the stoned corridor, he got a better look at his surroundings. He got the wounded boy up and they made their way out as well.

He heard yelling and cries mixed in with the gunfire coming from the stairwell and backed up. At a dead end on the other side, he turned to look for the crawlspace he spotted earlier when the men came to retrieve the other boy.

"Can you make it?" He asked the wounded kid, who nodded. "Here we go."

He hefted the boy up and watched as he used his good arm to pull himself all the way up. Following behind him, the boy tested the integrity of the small cavity. With a head nod, he signaled the wounded kid to start crawling. After about what seemed like half an hour, they came out on the other end of a corridor near the bottom of a stairwell. Another set of stairs went down to ground level and ahead of them was daylight.

Picking up the wounded kid, he carried him down the stairs and headed straight for the light. As soon as the desert air hit him, so did something else. His vision adjusted to see two of the men from earlier in front of him. The first one had a grin on his face while the other seemed sad.

"Not so fast, kiddo. This is the end of the line."

He felt pain spread through his chest and wetness. His knees became weak, and he forced them not to buckle under his own weight so not to drop the kid. The kid started screaming and wiggled his way out of his arms. Before he could get close to the men, the sad one aimed his gun and fired.

The kid went down hard, screaming more. The man stepped closer to him and fired another shot. Then the kid went still.

The helper boy fell to his knees. His voice seemed to not be working as he fought to speak and finally forced out one thing.

"Why?"

The grinning man gave a nod to the other one. He went to stand in front of him, the barrel of the gun close to his face.

"Welcome to your new home. Hell on Earth."

With that, the other man pulled the trigger. He watched helplessly as the bullet seemed to go in slow motion towards him before the round hit in the head.


"This is too fucking brutal, man," the one with the handgun said.

"It's not like we're actually killing them," the other one spat.

"Uh, yeah. We are. They're dead. We just killed a bunch of kids."

The other man gave him a nasty look and slung his assault rifle over his shoulder.

"Shut up and let's get going. Medical will be here for these two and into the regeneration chambers they go."

"Whatever. It still doesn't change the fact of what we just did."

The two men walked off, the man with the handgun taking a quick look back at the two bodies staining the desert floor.

*I'm so sorry.*

In a holding cell on the far side of the bunker, another set of twelve children sat huddled in fear. All except one. Vic Marzonetti was more angry than scared. The fact that someone had the audacity to invade his family's home and kidnap him was one reason. When he was being unloaded, it became clear to him those guys were not from a rival family. The other reason was that his friend, Eldan, who he liked very much also ended up in the room. And the state he was in made him want to tear someone's heart out.

Bandaged and bruised all over, Eldan lay fast asleep with his head in Vic's lap. The days in the cell did him no favors. Steady meals gave him enough strength to move around more. He wasn't sure who these people were. There would be hell to pay when everything was all over. Guaranteed. Eldan stirred as Vic stroked his hair. The blonde in certain parts had turned almost platinum. He wondered how that happened.

When the room began to crumble and shake, the children scurried. The door came toppling down and the first echoes of gunfire made them all stop in their tracks. Kidnapped in an unfamiliar place was bad enough. Going into a gunfight, not a smart idea. Some kids chanced it and headed out. Vic and Eldan waited until everyone else was gone before peeking out around the doorframe. As they eased closer to the stairs, they saw two of the kids taken out by gunmen below.

Scared and not ready to die, Vic, along with Eldan found an alternate route. They entered a crawlspace. Considering where it was located, they would end up on the same level as the gunmen. Further down, there was a large crack in the corner of a wall, and they could feel air when they stuck their hands in it. Going through, they ended up near a terrace on the outside and climbed down to the desert floor.

Open space spread before them. Eldan shook his head. They might as well have targets on their backs out there. A nearby stone overhead went through a section of the building. They ran through it.

Two men standing on the other side blocked their escape.

"Very clever. Too bad."

Before either boy could turn to make a run for it, they were shot. Vic felt the pain enter his chest as he watched Eldan get hit in the shoulder from turning. They both fell to the ground, Vic on his back, Eldan on his side. The man on the right stood over them, raising his gun to take aim.

"No! Please!" Vic cried as the man shot his friend again. He reached out towards him in vain. Then rage took over. "You sons of bitches!" He got halfway up when the man pulled the trigger again. The bullet hit him like a sledgehammer in the head.

Nothing.

From the command center, the four aliens watched the live feed of the holding cells. There were ten in all and watching how each child reacted to their situation, determined which trainer to pair them with. The methods were gruesome for a good reason.

"Why?" the coordinator cried out. "Why do such a thing?"

"Because," Karias answered, "we want them to know helplessness. To experience the pain of not being able to do anything."

"To think they have won when, in reality, they went straight to their doom," Lindo added.

"They're children!" The coordinator protested.

"Exactly." Telia relaxed in her floating seat. "By the time they come of age, this will have all meant nothing."

"And the next phase?"

"Will determine what humanity really entails," she answered.

The coordinator reared back in disgust. His grip on his tablet tightened as he spun around and headed out of the hangar.

"I think you may have hurt his," Attar frowned, thinking, "his feelings."

"How fragile can he be?" Telia waved a hand at him. "He knew what this program entailed. Did the humans think they could go head-to-head with Rellia without shedding blood and pride?"

On the feed, they saw the last two taken down in the sand. The female laughed when Vic, bleeding profusely from the first bullet wound, cursed his killers, then tried to attack the gunmen. Her expression grew serious as she eyed Karias sitting near to her. That boy definitely interested him.

"What ever would you do with such a creature?" She asked him.

He turned to her with a combined expression of elation and malice.

"Everything."

All four aliens leaned back and smiled as they continued to watch the cleanup.

The helper boy woke up and immediately gasped for air as he realized he was indeed alive. As proof, he could still feel the pain where the bullets hit. Running his hands across where the wounds would be, he felt nothing. Not a scratch or a scar. He bolted upright and pulled his shirt up to inspect his chest. No indication of harm marked him anywhere.

Fearful, he looked for the wounded kid and found him sleeping on the floor close to him. He crawled over and checked for any signs of damage.

The wounded kid was no longer wounded. It wasn't just the gunshot wounds gone. His eye, arm and legs were pristine. A closer inspection of the kid's face showed he was still in pain. He'd already been through enough and now being shot on top of it.

*This kid can't get a break.*

Then he cursed inwardly. They were back in a holding cell. This time it was a wooden enclosure, not stone. And no windows. The headcount was the same with a few other different kids. The bully was back, and he sat against the wall on the other side, glaring at him and the sleeping kid. With a stare, he dared the bully to try getting at the kid. As everyone woke up, the crying started.

Two days into their new lease on life and all the children were forcing themselves to eat all the meals sent through. Their appetites went the moment they all found themselves still in the clutches of the enemy. For the first time, the helper kid paused his spoon before shoving it in his mouth.

*What were they feeding us?*

He figured it had to be some kind of nutrient packed stuff because the amount of energy he felt after eating was odd. It was especially noticeable in the now healed kid. The sheer force he applied when ramming the bully into the wall negated his physical appearance. Remembering his situation, he shrugged and continued eating. At least it was good.

Vic Marzonetti woke up fighting invisible demons. Eldan pushed him back to the floor to calm him down and held him there. When he finally settled, he stared into his friend's grey eyes that glinted silver. He reached up to caress his cheek. Eldan slapped his hand to the side and glared at him before moving away.

He sighed and flung an arm over his eyes.

*Pretty sure I was dead.*

With his other hand, he checked his body and couldn't feel any marks where the bullets went through. That frightened him. And he could still feel the pain. Not a little bit, a lot. Like someone had only triaged then him sent home. Moving his arm from his eyes, he looked over at Eldan. Pain etched his entire face.

Around the room, he saw some kids he didn't recognize. Sitting up, he turned towards the wall and tapped it. Solid wood. Sniffles started again, making him angry at the ones doing it. Crying won't solve anything. Eldan seemed to feel the same by the look on his face as he glanced around the room.

By the second day, he was wondering for what purpose they were all brought there. They were being well fed and kept out of the elements. Granted, they had been killed once. Again, no one spoke. The food arrived and doled out as usual. He wanted answers.

And on the fifth day came a voice booming through hidden speakers in the holding cells.

"Wake up, my pets," the soothing female voice said. "Time for you to prove how worthy you are to me."

Inside the holding cells, all the children looked around, trying to find out where the voice was coming from. Fear gripped them.

"I will let go half the children in your group."

There were sounds of relief and salvation.

"But you must fight for it."

That stomped their hope.

"I will determine your worth by who is still in that room and who will fight to get out."

The locking mechanism on the doors released.

"Show me how much you want to live."

The bully in the holding cell with the helper wasted no time, punching and kicking his way towards them. Two other kids jumped him, and he was having a hard time getting them off. One kid crawled away, trying to sneak past without engaging. A kid using both hands like a hammer into his back brought him down. The helper heard the contact and winced. Then another kid came at that one.

An arm came around the helper kid's neck and pulled him to the floor. He positioned his elbow near the kid's kidney. When they landed, his elbow went down into his assailant, who yelled in pain. Getting up, he saw his ward pummeling another who had attached himself to his legs. After the fifth blow to the head, the kid slumped down in a heap and the not wounded kid backed away. He nodded towards him, then the door.

The helper kid, being closest to it, swung it open and looked both ways down the corridor. Seeing it clear, he motioned for the not wounded kid to join him. One kid had already gone out and from behind him, he saw one more getting up from putting another kid to the mat. As they fled, looking back, they saw the most frightening thing.

Still on the ground and in obvious pain, the little one who had tried to sneak away grabbed the bully's ankle as he walked past and brought him down to his level. His hands went around the bully's neck. Using all his body weight, he applied pressure. The bully tried in vain to get up.

Each time he got a few inches off the floor, the little one would slam him back down. After doing that a few times, the bully went still. His body had lost color. Satisfied, the little one crawled to the open door.

Mesmerized as they were, the helper and the not wounded kid briefly stopped moving then hurried out.

The expression on the little kid's face was something unholy. Another kid behind the little one jumped over him and ran past them down the corridor.

As soon as someone threw the first punch, Vic Marzonetti grabbed Eldan and headed for the door. He didn't want to fight a bunch of scared kids his own age. No. He wanted the bastards who kidnapped them. The assholes who shot him. Halfway across the room, two of the other kids blocked their path.

"Oh, hell no," the first yelled.

"You don't get to get out of here like you're special," the other one said.

They came at them like animals. His friend cried out in pain as the one on him bit him in the thigh while trying to tackle him. Enraged, Eldan grabbed the kid by the hair and kneed him repeatedly in the face. Blood flew everywhere. Then he dropped the kid like a sack of garbage and continued to the door. Vic grappled with his opponent and tossed him farther into the room. The kid hit the wall with a loud thud.

Flinging open the door, the two made their way down the nearby staircase. Once again, they found themselves heading out towards daylight. Just outside the installation, a group of adults attacked the children who converged. One of them was the gunman from before with the assault rifle.

"Still not your day, kid."

His fists were like boulders as he struck Vic. No matter which way he dodged, the man's blows connected, and he had no opportunity to fight back. The last blow got him in the face and his head snapped back. He saw a blazing sun before everything went dark. Again.

⌐

Damon woke up inside the regeneration chamber and stared at the ceiling as its shield retracted. Not quite calm, he slowly exhaled. His body felt like it had been in a meat grinder, the pain in his limbs from pushing them too far lingering. He mentally cursed every person who forced him to the facility.

The soldiers who picked a fight ended up having their asses handed to them. Him being the only one disciplined; the commander telling him he should know how to restrain himself. The commander and his cronies who stood by, letting his squad throw him a blanket party in the middle of the night then shipping him out.

There were two choices on the table for him: the brig or retraining. He never got to choose. Another commander had come in while they deliberated and suggested this place. The moment he set foot on the desert floor; he knew this was no retraining ground. His life would end in that bunker. The barcode attached to him correlated with the prison system and that course. No normal human being could get through that.

*I'm a guinea pig.*

Apparently, he wasn't the only one who made it through the course in record time. Whispers spread about another soldier, angrier and more prone to violence. His outburst brought him under the tutelage of some dude named Lindo. Somewhat tall with sandy brown hair and eyes to match (which were so stunning by the female nurses' standards), he had also been put down by medical as he exited the course. It took a lot more personnel to do it.

A face loomed over Damon, then a bright light shined in his eyes. Startled, he scooted up out of the chamber bed and knocked away whoever stood close. He could hear more footsteps surrounding him in the commotion.

His vision had not returned to normal. Even when he squinted, it didn't correct itself.

"Calm down, soldier! Everything's fine."

"Fuck you! No, it's not!"

He struggled when four men tried to subdue him while another loaded an injection gun. The man turned to him with a malicious smile. He felt fear for a split second, then rage took over. Before the man could get close enough to use it, Damon brought his arms together, smashing his restrainers into each other. He heard their heads hit, then flung them off. His target was the door behind the man with the injection gun.

With lightning speed, he made a dash for it, ignoring the screaming from his muscles. He got to the threshold on the other side when a fist rammed into his kidney. It felt like a sledgehammer, and he coughed up blood.

*Fuck! Fuck!*

As he slid to the floor, he caught sight of an enormous man with strange golden eyes staring down at him, amused. He knelt next to Damon.

"You're a feisty one, hmm? We'll start your training next week."

The giant turned to the man with the injection gun and nodded towards him. He felt the needle stab him and the curtains closed fast around him as he fell into a deep sleep again. Before it took him completely, he had a revelation.

*Aliens.*

‿

The first group of trainees climbed up the side of the mountain from the forest floor, hoping for salvation at the top. Each trainer had sent their best for this exercise and waited leisurely for them to crest over the ledge at the platform. Two years of harsh treatment and out of the one hundred and twenty, only about eighty-two remained. The ones who didn't make the cut got patched up, mind swiped and left in the vicinity of their snatch site.

This is where the organization's connections with law enforcement came in handy. No one was the wiser where the abducted children had been all this time. Representatives shut news media outlets out of reporting the incidents and threatened the parents into silence. Everything was going according to protocol.

A trainer saw his trainee struggling up the rope, still a good distance down. The kid had lost his grip previously and slid down. From his position up top, his trainer could see the rope burns on his hands. He contemplated if he should let the boy up or not. Off to his left, he saw another trainer step towards the ledge as a hand come clambering over.

The trainee pulled himself onto the platform, sweaty and exhausted. Breathing heavy, a rasping coming from his lips, he looked up with a sigh of relief. His trainer lifted one foot and planted it square on the trainee's chest and kicked him right over the ledge.

"Not good enough," the trainer called down to the soldier in free fall.

"You know he'll probably land badly and break every bone in his body," the observing trainer said.

"That's what the regeneration chamber is for. After all this time, they should know better than to think it would be this easy."

"They're looking for the light at the end of the tunnel." The other trainer gave him a sour look.

"Is that what you wished when we were in training?"

"Is this not it?" He replied.

The other trainer snorted and looked down, letting the zooming lenses adjust.

"This is hell on Earth. If you think this is the light, I may have to put you down myself sooner than later."

"Oh?"

Both trainers stood side by side, playfully glaring at each other.

The helper kid watched the other who had made it to the ledge come plummeting down screaming. It solidified his feelings that this was another exercise in torture disguised as a training lesson to push their bodies. At sixteen, he was very aware of how his own had changed since coming to the bunker.

Not overly bulky, he had well-defined ripped muscles. At which point he actually asked his trainer if he could get leaner instead. The answer came in a headlock, followed by a knife slicing through his gut. The man was temperamental at best.

A few yards ahead lay the wounded boy from the holding cell. They had shoved him off twice, resulting in his hands and body bloody. Instead of falling all the way down, they had both figured out how to grab hold of the rope during free fall. He marveled at the other kid's speed even in his state.

*Guess I better up my game.*

He had defended the kid when he felt brave and paid the price for it. He knew having attachments was a no-no but couldn't help falling in love with him. That's what he felt. Being young didn't make him stupid and not understand his own feelings. Whether or not it was mutual didn't matter. He would be his guardian in the shadows for as long as it took.

Back over the ledge for the third time, he braced himself for the push off. In the corner of his vision, he saw the wounded kid's trainer grab him by the hair and punch him in the face, letting him drop to the ground.

He clenched his fists, angry that the trainers knew they couldn't fight back in their current condition. A darkness loomed over him, and he stared up into his trainer's face.

All lean muscle with straight dark hair, wearing a suit, the man oozed sadistic malice. His eyes twinkled with glee as he clearly thought about what to do to him next. He glanced over at the wounded kid on the ground, then back at him.

*Shit!*

He must have seen him do it earlier. The trainer grabbed him by the collar of his shirt and lifted him off the ground by a few inches. Where that kind of strength came from, the helper boy couldn't imagine. Their eyes locked.

"Feeling heroic?"

He struggled a bit to stop his neck from being squeezed so he could answer.

"Not at all."

"You want some of that? We can arrange it. Of course," his trainer's eyes went sinister, "we would watch. Entertainment is scarce these days."

Horrified, the helper grabbed hold of the hand holding him up and tried to break free. His trainer must have understood the look on his face because he started laughing. Tears formed in the corner of his eyes as he kept on, while not letting go of the helper boy. When he finally finished laughing, he glared at the boy.

"You want to hate me? Here's a reason. Enjoy."

With that, he tossed the helper boy over the ledge. This time far enough away from the rope so that he couldn't catch it. He knew it would hurt worse than anything he had ever felt so far. The closer he got to the forest floor, he calculated when to brace for impact. The only thing he could do now was to lessen the damage.

His trainer turned to the other and pointed at the unconscious kid at their feet. The other trainer cocked his head and thought for a moment. Then he nodded, and they both looked down at the kid like a piece of meat.

The second group of climbers included Eldan and Vic. So far, they were both sent hurdling down twice because Vic couldn't stand seeing his friend get punished at the top. He would lunge at his friend's trainer to stop the assault, only to be beaten himself and tossed over. On the third try, he decided it was indeed a lost cause and no matter what happened this time, he would be still and do nothing.

On the platform, his trainer stared down at him, waiting. Off to the left, Eldan lay on the ground exhausted, unable to fight. That didn't stop his trainer from getting down on one knee and using one arm on the ground as leverage, punched him repeatedly. There was no anger or malice on the trainer's face. Nothing at all. It was just a random act of violence to let out his own demons.

Vic's trainer kept watch on him and when he didn't move, his trainer smiled.

"Learned your lesson? Good."

He grabbed Vic by the head and made sure they were eye to eye. His hands twisted. He heard a tiny snap before everything went black.

Cries of agony echoed from outside the bay doors, each one followed by the sound of crashing. Telia, now known as Celestial Mother, raised her head to see what the commotion was all about.

It had been years since someone had been bold enough to invade the space her companions and she populated in their command center. Many of the candidates snatched up at the tender age of preteen years were now nearing adulthood.

From the other side of the doors, she heard a loud cracking sound and saw hairline fractures appear diagonally across it. The doors parted until fingers were visible, prying it open. One of the candidate's contorted face emerged as the gap became wide enough for him to get through. She remembered him. The small child left crawling on the floor during the initial trials. He was no longer small, standing at six feet two inches tall, all lean muscles and angrier than she had ever seen him.

He let out a horrendous yell and flash stepped towards the aliens. Karias met him halfway, blocking his advance. The sheer force of the boy's hit pushed him back. Surprised, he repositioned himself and braced for a second assault. The boy came at him, veering to the right at the last nanosecond and going straight for Attar. Hatred oozed from every pore.

Her mate, surprised, barely had time to dodge him. He flipped backwards off his cushioned seat and landed on the wall behind him. As the boy readjusted for another attack, her mate launched from the wall and rammed into the boy. Amazingly, the boy took the hit and only moved an inch back. A blurring whirlwind of blows ensued as the two engaged in one-on-one combat. When the boy came flying out, correcting his body midflight he landed on his feet, skidding back to a stop then immediately lunged forward.

She had seen enough.

Jumping down from her seat, she got between the two and moved to stop him. Which didn't work as planned. In his ferocity, the boy was like a battering ram with suped up power. His strength amazed and terrified her. The hit she received made her eyes widen and knew she was in trouble. He stopped his advance and looked around. His eyes moved at rapid speed, scanning the room in mere seconds. She knew what he sought.

He was one of the children they had trained to wield the special swords. An apt pupil, he excelled at it; frighteningly so. There was only one other on par with him, and the aliens felt unsure if teaching their techniques was a good idea. She didn't want incidents like this to become common, and hated hurting the fragile creatures any more than their trainers already did.

"Don't let him move!"

The other three converged on the boy just as he pivoted and made his way to the wall of katanas. Halfway there, Karias brought his hands together, forming a hammer and slammed down on his back. The boy went down hard to the floor. He got right back up and fought each one, holding his own against them. Frustrated at not being able to stop him, all four aliens hit him at once.

His body had already showed signs of massive damage. Blood was everywhere, every drop his. Yet, he still fought as if he was immune to pain and the truth be told, they conditioned him that way.

He hit the floor again, this time forming a crater from the impact. A loud crunching sound filled the room. Eyes still fueled with rage, he tried to reach out with a mangled arm. The desperation making his movements seem like stop motion.

Celestial Mother bent down beside him and caressed his forehead. The look of disgust on his face before his arm dropped and his eyes slowly closed saddened her. A sense of remorse gripped her.

Soldiers came pouring into the command center and four of them stepped up to the boy's body.

"Don't touch him!" She roared.

They all stopped dead in their tracks, afraid. Confused

by her anger. Attar frowned and looked away. She turned to him.

"Explain this!"

When he didn't answer, continuing to avert his gaze, she snatched him by the front of his robes and drew him in close. She bared her teeth as he tried to flinch away. When he couldn't get out of her grip, he relented.

"I had his trainers give him special treatment during a test. He was being violent, so we agreed to teach him a lesson in true violence. He must have just awakened from the regeneration chamber."

"What did you do?" Her anger so palpable even the other two aliens backed away.

"As I said…" her throttling him by the neck cut him off. When she stopped, he finished. "We tore his limbs off."

The female alien's face went pale, and she dropped her mate as if he were something foul. She went over to the boy, lifeless on the floor in a pool of his own blood. A medical team arrived, along with the coordinator. He took one look and made a disapproving face.

"Fix him," she commanded. "Then send him back."

The coordinator balked.

"We can't do that." Her eyes glowed. He backed away. "He knows too much. It's best if we dispose of the body."

She stood to her full height and stared down at him.

"You will do what I ask, human." She said calmly, her true intent clear.

The coordinator gulped and nodded his head. While the medical team attached tubes to the boy's body and loaded it on the stretcher that floated upwards, her eyes never wavered from him. Such a quiet child with darkness lurking beneath the surface, brought out by the training.

The scientists on hand created a drug that suppressed

it when he wasn't doing drills and another to put him in a deep sleep during lights out.

"Make sure he's okay for a while. We will bring him back into the fold when he is able."

"Of course. If that's what you want."

"As you say, he knows too much." She turned to her seat and leaped up. "And, as volatile as he is, we may need him in the future."

Settling back into her cushioned seat, she stared down at her mate. A better leash was in order, so that wouldn't happen again.

Hana ran to his office in a state of despair after seeing the feed from the command room. His heart beated so fast he shifted into female form when he tried to calm himself. Gasping for air, Hana clutched the front of her shirt, the other hand on the desk holding her up.

Someone suddenly blocked the light in the room and spun Hana around from behind. Sgt. Mitchum grabbed her by the shoulders and pushed her into the nearby wall. He yanked her pants down far enough for him to use his legs to stomp them to the floor.

"No." Hana tried to plead with her gaze. "Not here."

He held her face in his hands and kissed her hard, pulling on her bottom lips as he disengaged. His breath was super-heated.

"Here," he rasped. "Now."

She felt him enter her with desperate force and let out a cry she could no longer contain. Her arms wrapped around his back and hooked over his shoulders as she muffled her cries into his shirt. They ended up sliding to the floor, his thrusts relentless despite their position. Hana gripped tighter.

She submitted to his wants. The only solace she could have right now. The images of all the recruits she'd witnessed in training haunted her. Even her orgasm didn't erase them.

*Was I wrong to be here?*

In the dead of night, the dark car slowed to a stop to minimize the noise near a dirt road. Up ahead was a boarding house for boys that the organization had established without government knowledge. A nonprofit entity, it helped the needy and gave shelter to wayward children.

Two men exited the car and opened the trunk. They lifted the young boy out and gently laid him down in the grass at the edge of the property. A light rain came and gave a sheen to the boy's exposed pristine skin. Not a scar was present anywhere on him.

"Live a bit, kid. You've earned it," the man said as he patted him on the head.

"Damn shame," the other man said.

"Yeah, that was seriously fucked up."

The first man looked up at the sky as the rain got a little harder.

"Think he'll be okay out here?"

"Yep. Phone call was made, message sent. They'll find him within the next twenty minutes."

After the first man closed the trunk, and they both got in the front seat of the car. The driver saw a light come on in the house and let out a sigh of relief. The walk to the end of the driveway took a good seven-minutes, which meant the boy would be safe inside sooner than planned. Putting the car in drive, he eased back onto the road, headlights still off until they got far enough away for it to be safe to turn them on.

## IMPLEMENTATION

Flawless skin, full lips, and an innocence ripe for corruption. At nineteen and a half, the new office clerk proved an anomaly. Fresh from officer's school, the young man had tested high for the armed forces and fast tracked. Chad Hoskins recognized the plant from the get-go. *Goddamn!* He could smell the kid a mile away, kicking out pheromones at high levels.

*One of those damned Biodes.*

His father hated those things with a passion, and he, too, had adopted similar feelings. All of that went out the window as the young soldier purposely walked past him to get to his desk. It was only a matter of time before they would end up alone together for some unforeseen reason. Hoskins Jr. laughed inwardly. He would play the game and find out who was pulling the baby spy's strings.

In his private office, Chad looked up the soldier's stats and snorted. Mediocre in shooting, proficient, not great, at hand-to-hand combat and good with tactics. Combined, none of it made sense. To him, it reeked of miscommunication. From the side window of his office, he had a view of him at the well-organized yet cluttered desk. The boy's placement, failed at its proposed subtlety. He believed they had messed up. An empty desk farther down sat out of his line of sight.

He sat back in his chair and thought about how he should play this thing.

How would they arrange their potential meet?

Whoever orchestrated this obviously put some planning into it. While he tapped a pen on his desk, Chad smiled. He sat up and pushed up from his chair. Outside his door, he watched the soldier pretend to scour the data on his touchscreen, then proceeded to him.

"Morning, soldier."

The young man jumped up from his seat, startled and stammered out a reply.

"Good, good morning, sir. Officer Eric Brenner reporting for duty, sir."

He retroactively gave a salute.

Chad waved a hand.

"No need for that in this office. Sit."

"Yes, sir." Brenner obeyed and sat, waiting.

"I just wanted to welcome you to the fold. We run a tight ship here."

"So I've heard," the young man paused. "Sir."

"Now, we gotta' stop that." Chad gave him a winning smile. "How about we go get a drink later and shoot the shit?"

"I'm not old enough to drink yet." Brenner stopped before finishing.

Chad knew he was about to add 'sir' again.

"Well, I figured that, kid. You can still drink soda, can't you?"

The young man blushed with embarrassment.

Chad's heart did a funny thing in his chest. His groin tightened, and he found himself staring at those full pink lips, wishing they were around the rim of his cock.

*Definitely a plant.*

Chad decided this could be fun. His father would shit a brick if he found out.

*Fuck it.*

How many chances does one get to personally desecrate

a Bi-Genetic? It was the perfect opportunity to find out if any of the rumors about them were true.

"Sorry, I didn't mean to offend you."

"Not at all, kid. We punch out at nineteen thirty. See you then."

As he turned and walked away, he saw the young soldier get out of his seat again.

"Yes, sir."

In his office, Chad grinned.

The watcher sat on the opposite end of the room, rummaging through files and recorded the interaction between Hoskins Jr. and their agent. His organization knew the man was no dummy and was confident that he would make the first move. No need to overthink the mission this time. He felt a sense of dread and sadness for the young soldier, knowing what horrors he might encounter being with Chad. It was for the good of humanity. Still, it left a foul taste in his mouth.

One of the youngest doctors in the region at twenty-one, the newbie had an ego to match. Tall, drop dead gorgeous and an I.Q. nearly off the charts, the man could do no wrong. His bedside manner bordered on silent seduction. He never raised his voice, even during surgery, and talked smoothly, calmly. He seemed to never be in a rush, yet finished everything he did in record time. His precision with a scalpel made other doctors squirm with envy.

The head of the pediatrics department fumed at the thought of being forced to put the young doctor on his team for a one-year stint. He knew well that the numbers were not up to snuff, so he tried his best to run clean with a swamped staff. One more doctor wouldn't make a difference in his book. The chairman of the board felt otherwise. Another factor was that he just didn't like the kid. He stood at the triage station, lost in thought until he heard inaudible whispers and gasps. Looking up, his worst nightmare had arrived.

Dark hair, thick and wavy, rested on the shoulders of the white lab coat. Perfectly moisturized skin and a devious smile complemented the well-shaped lips. Eyes the color of a storming sea stared straight ahead, not wavering to acknowledge the attention. He was close to six feet four inches tall and even through the dress slacks, one could tell how lean and muscular he was. His stride was one with purpose, making a beeline right for the head of pediatrics.

"Good morning, Doctor Allan. I'm Doctor Winston Sterling."

*What kind of pompous name is that?* Dr. Allan thought as he frowned.

"I look forward to working with you and your team." He held out a hand for him to shake.

Dr. Allan didn't take it and stood up to his full height of six feet. He had to look up a bit to make sure he conveyed authority. Sharp gasps erupted at his blatant disrespect for a colleague.

"This isn't a pony ride, Doctor," he said. The last he spat out vehemently. "I don't care how many fawn over you or how great they praise your talents. We are on the front line of new life."

Dr. Sterling dropped his hand to his side and stared at him. Something changed in those stormy eyes and Dr. Allan stepped away in fear. Nothing. As blank as paper, the young doctor seemed to stare into the abyss.

"I understand. That's why I'm here. I hope we can save more wonderful lives together."

His uplifting voice had some of the staff making

baby sounds. A smile crossed his deadpan expression. One that left the head of pediatrics cold inside. Suddenly, it all went away, and Sterling returned to being a regular guy again. He turned away from him and proceeded to introduce himself to each staff member.

*What kind of monster is he?* Dr. Allan asked himself.

Dr. Sterling made his rounds, getting acquainted with the area and staff while surveying every corner of the wing. He just wasn't there to help. No. There was something very wrong going on at that hospital. The other reason was to have an ally within the city if one of the organization's agents ended up in the emergency room. His current assignment was pediatrics while still on call for general ER. The head of the department wouldn't be a problem, so he had dismissed the man from his report.

From his lab coat pocket, he brought out a piece of wrapped candy and twirled it between his thumb and index finger. The organization specially made them for him to ease the phantom random pains that surfaced. Right now, he felt the tingling. A precursor to the searing agony that would bring him to his knees. Unwrapping the sweet and sour treat, he popped it in his mouth and let the medication do its job.

He went inside his patient's room and sat down in the chair beside the bed. The new mother, exhausted and happy, cradled her newborn child. When she looked up, her eyes widened in surprise, and she blushed.

"How are you doing today?" he asked.

"Fine, now that you're here." She sounded like a schoolgirl confessing to her crush.

"Good."

A twinge of pain hit him hard, and he stiffened, letting it subside. It lasted a mere moment. He didn't let her see it, continuing to smile as she praised how well behaved her baby was. He barely heard her. Inside, he felt the rage creeping.

*One day.*

⤳

Once again, Celestial Mother heard the telltale sounds of combat outside the command center doors, and this time, she knew who was coming. She glanced over at Karias and smirked.

*All yours.*

He made a sideways glance at the doors as they burst open and fell into four pieces, each section cut with precision. Vic Marzonetti stood with one of the special katanas held in his grip. From the beads of sweat on his face, it was clearly too much for him to handle. It got him to where he intended, his fierce hatred visible.

Karias leaped down from his cushioned floating seat and waited for the young man to come at him. Instead, Marzonetti shifted to one side and did the same. A stalemate. Not one to be toyed with, Karias sped forward. The young man's face contorted in agreement, and they clashed with a loud ringing as their swords met and snapped in half. Tossing the broken weapons aside, the two engaged in battle.

To his surprise, Karias found the young man faster than him and barely had time to block every hit delivered. From the outside, it looked like a haze of swirling tornadoes, and he marveled at the tactics the human implemented.

Distracted by his observations, he left an opening and Marzonetti took advantage. The hit was brutal and sent Karias sailing across the room. As he landed against the wall, he heard a loud crack and knew something had broken inside of him.

The other three came down, surrounding him like a barricade. Celestial Mother stared at the human in anger.

"What is the meaning of this?" She demanded.

Marzonetti stood breathing heavily, foam seeping from his mouth through gritted teeth. He sucked in a deep breath and finally answered.

"I am leaving. I will not let you do anymore to me."

"Oh?"

"And I'm taking Eldan with me. I won't let him stay here one moment longer."

"Or what, dear child?"

Marzonetti face scrunched up worse than before.

"I will kill everyone."

From the look in his eyes, Karias knew he meant every word. He could see Celestial Mother thinking when there was nothing to think about. They had no intention of taming that boy and having him start killing mass amounts of people was not an option. She seemed to get the situation as well and stepped forward.

"And what will you do? Where will you go?"

"Home."

Celestial Mother laughed. It rang out through the room, bouncing off the metal walls.

"So be it."

She was on him in a flash, sword to his neck, and the color drained from him. He went rigid as he realized his position was reversed.

"Don't think I won't remember this day," she sneered. "Get him out of my sight."

A group of soldiers appeared from the other side of the room and Marzonetti let them seize him. He had a look of relief on his face, followed by his body finally shutting down from the amount of energy he had exerted. His body went limp, and two soldiers draped his arms around their necks to drag him out.

For weeks, Vic watched and listened to his family go about their routines. He had no reason to announce his return yet and was glad he hadn't done so when he came back into town. His father, always the one to dote on him, had moved on as if he meant nothing. At first, he was angry, then remembered what kind of family it was. Hateful, greedy, narcissistic, and non-too loyal. Of the five major crime families, his was next to the worst.

Beside him in the stolen vehicle, Eldan rested against the passenger side window. He did that a lot, going into a state of oblivion to block out the occasional episodes of pain. Strikingly beautiful, Eldan's sleeping face angelic. His blonde hair had gone stark white from the massive trauma endured through training. Combined with his silver eyes, he looked other worldly.

A short, dark-haired wig lay in his lap. To avoid standing out too much, they opted to go in disguise. He even had contacts because those eyes gave him away. Enchanting even incognito. Vic wanted him so badly it hurt. Now was not the time. Not yet.

The listening device squawked, and he adjusted the frequency. His father's right-hand men were in his office. A meeting had been called.

"Heard something strange along the pipeline, boss," one of his men said.

"Ah yeah? What you hear?"

"Some kid running around looks like yours been asking questions."

"That right?" There were loud crackling sounds. He knew from memory that his father enjoyed eating hard-shelled nuts. "What's this boy asking?"

"Stuff like what jobs we're doing and what not."

"I don't like that. Get rid of him."

Vic jolted upright in the driver's seat.

"What if he really is your son?"

"The fuck do I care? He didn't do anything to further the family, so it doesn't matter if he's dead or alive."

"What about your legacy, boss?"

"Pfft! I ain't dead yet. There's plenty of pretty young things to knock up if I need more of my seed spread."

"In that case," another of his men piped in, "I got some prospects for ya.'"

He laughed and his men followed suit. When they finished, his father cleared his throat.

"Make sure you do this clean. I don't want anyone knowing he ever resurfaced."

"You got it, boss," his men replied in unison.

Inside the car, Vic fumed. He resolved to let them off easy. Even if it took years, he was going to usurp his father's power and make a name for himself. Beside him, Eldan was awake and, by the look on his face, had also been listening. Those eyes held malice. Since getting conked out months ago and left for dead on the side of the road twelve miles from where they were abducted, the two found each other and inseparable since. Eldan became something of a bodyguard even though he could defend himself just as well.

"Gearing for a takeover?" Eldan asked softly.

"Oh, I can do better than that," he answered.

"Timeline?"

"Let's have a bit of fun."

Eldan's face twitched and a tiny smile curved the corners of his mouth, then disappeared. That made Vic angry. It resulted from the training. None of them would ever be the same. The way Eldan carried himself lately made him think something had broken inside. Irreparable.

With his surveillance lenses at max zoom, the watcher assigned to Vic Marzonetti, kept vigil over the car and the homestead. He, too, had a listening device and heard every word from both sides. The spies within the organization in charge of manipulating events had already set things in motion, and he knew the kid wasn't aware of what would happen. The watcher had full knowledge of what his takeover entailed.

*God help us all.*

He smirked thinking about it. With aliens and everything else going on, he still clung to a faith he now had doubts about. Old habits die hard. To complete the phrase, he made the sign of the cross, touching forehead, chest and both shoulders before kissing his two fingers up to the heavens.

◠

Police stations had a stench Damon found unappealing. Burnt coffee, stale sugar from hours old donuts and desperation. In a nice suit and tie, he sat waiting in the chief's office for the man to show up. Seven minutes late. He didn't like unpunctuality. Time was precious. A quick survey of the room made him want to run from this place.

The door opened. A barrel-chested man in an equally well tailored suit entered. He had dark short hair peppered with grey and small craters along his cheeks. In one hand was a mug of said burnt coffee and in the other was a tablet displaying his personal file. The chief plopped down in his chair and set his items aside. Black sludge swayed in the mug. Damon's stomach lurched.

"Well, I see you're one of those smart asses who tested high. Going straight to detective rank. No job experience."

Damon wasn't sure if he was supposed to answer that, so kept quiet.

"Not much of a talker, huh?"

The chief grimaced and took a sip of his coffee.

"I didn't know it was a question. Sorry."

The chief set his mug down and glared at him.

"You really are a smart ass. Let me tell you something." He pointed a finger at him as he began talking.

Damon fought back the urge to roll his eyes upward. *Good gravy!*

He tuned out the chief's rantings and reached in his pocket for the pack of chewing gun given to him by the organization. He tossed a piece in his mouth, biting down into the hard shell. Tasting the bitter soft center made him squeeze his eyes shut.

"Did you just put gum in your mouth?"

The chief's voice grated as it cut through the fog in his head.

"Yes, sir. Mouth felt a bit dry."

"Were you listening to me?" The chief roared.

"Absolutely." The man's frown deepened. "Sir."

"Get out of my office!"

He stood, still pointing, this time at the door behind him. Damon sighed and got up, leaving the small room.

On the main floor, all the workers had stopped what they were doing to glance at the office and watch him emerge. Some seemed curious while others, particularly the uniforms, gave him that look. The one that said he didn't belong here and there would be no friends to back him up.

*Ain't that the truth?*

He proceeded to the empty desk with his name plaque on it and stared down at the baby pacifier with a box of wet naps beside it. Snickers erupted around him. He kicked the bottom drawer, and it popped open with a loud clang, causing everyone to jump. He slid the items in then kicked it closed before sitting down.

"Hey!" An officer a few desks down from him yelled.

"Some of us have to work. Keep that shit down."

Everyone averted strange stares at him and he wondered what they were waiting for. A fight? Submission? They would get neither. He ignored the man and turned on his touchscreen. The logo for the department flipped around in the middle of it.

Drug Enforcement.

*Great.*

"Did you hear me, newbie?" The officer had stood up from his desk to approach him.

*Shit! Really?*

"You better answer when someone's talking to you."

He calculated the distance of the officer approaching his desk. As he crossed the threshold of his space, Damon stood, pushing the desk forward with his pelvis and sent it right into the officer. The man went flying backwards into the desk catty corner from his and people made loud hisses and 'ohs'.

*Yeah, that had to hurt.*

"Oh, damn!" He said in mocked concern. "You alright, pal?"

He went to see if he could help. Another detective stopped him.

"Don't worry about it. We got this. Not your fault. These desks are shit and there's no sign of a budget for new equipment coming soon."

Damon looked around and confirmed the office area was indeed lacking.

"Plus, that guy's an asshole." His eyes went wide with disbelief, and the detective let out a loud guffaw. "Detective James," he said, holding out a hand.

"Damon Peterson," he replied, shaking it. "Good to meet you. Does that apply to the chief, too?"

"Oh, more than you know," Detective James said.

"Be careful. Newbies tend to get the shaft around here."

"For how long?"

A female uniform came around the desks and slapped Damon on the back.

"Maybe a year or two." She smiled, then winked.

Another detective on the other side raised his coffee mug at him in salute.

*Fuck my life.*

The taste of stale, stiff gum evaded his senses and he spit it out into the trash can under his desk. His stint of drug busts and reports had begun.

Guns were a necessary tool of trade for any assassin. What kind and its style depended on the wielder. The organization's chief buyer had found an underground gunsmith who didn't have any moral compass when creating his wares. A perfect scenario in his book. He strolled down the cobblestoned street and turned into a narrow alley. An entrance appeared at the end on the left. An old metal door retrofitted with three locks, and he guessed they were probably deadbolts.

He did the coded knock and heard the locks being slammed open from the other side. The door creaked open, and he stepped into a dimly lit foyer. A young boy of maybe twelve ushered him in, then re-bolted the door. Only one was a deadbolt.

The boy led him down the hall, through a wooden door and down into the basement. Bright light assaulted him as he stepped into the workshop.

At the bench sat a man in his early forties engraving the side of a small arm's piece. His focus was intense as the buyer watched the magnified eye go unblinking. The gunsmith finally sat up straight and turned to him. He lifted the eyepiece up away from his face.

"What you want from me?" His accent was thick.

"I have business for you."

"A piece?" The gunsmith seemed disappointed.

"Not a piece. Long term. Many, many pieces."

That perked the gunsmith right up, and his eyes beamed. The buyer had researched the man. He received random small commissions, mostly vanity pieces. Enough money for food and shelter most of the time, but he still struggled. With a small son to take care of, he longed for more work. The buyer pulled out the mini dossiers and set them in front of the gunsmith.

"I need you to make special guns for these people."

"How special?"

"You can incorporate color in the metal."

The gunsmith always wanted to experiment with making vibrant metals that showed off his talent. He suddenly frowned.

"How much?"

Customers had cheated the man on pricing many times before because of his unknown status. Most people in the area went to the bigger smiths when they wanted a piece made. The buyer found their craftsmanship lacking. They were nothing like what this man could do.

"Five thousand each."

The man's eyes widened, and he leaned forward.

"How many?"

The buyer tapped the stack of dossiers. There were at least twenty.

"And there will be more to come over the next decade."

"How much time to do jobs?"

"However long it takes. They need to be perfect."

The gunsmith grinned.

"I do perfect."

When the buyer left after two hours of conversation with the gunsmith, he headed back down the street.

He took out his cell phone and typed in the confirmation code. Someone would anonymously deliver the guns to the recipients as needed. He eagerly waited to see the first ones.

⤿

Chad Hoskins wasted no time in claiming the young soldier. Not even six months after his first day at the office, Brenner had already been going out with him every weekend. Whenever he tried to engage in conversation with him, Chad shut that down with short, simple answers.

Impatient, and ready to have some fun with his new plaything, Hoskins proposed marriage, knowing the little spy would say yes like the good soldier he was. At dinner to celebrate, he broke down the rules.

"Now," Chad began, wiping his mouth with his napkin. "At the office, you are just another body to punch the clock and crunch numbers. You bet not ever show up there in female form."

Eric stopped eating; the soup spoon held midair.

"Okay," he said.

"I mean it." Chad pointed a finger at him. "At home, I don't ever want to see you like this. Got me?" Eric nodded. "Good. My father don't like your kind and we don't want to give him any reasons to blow your head off or have you dissected."

Eric blanched and set his spoon down in the bowl. Chad smiled inwardly. It was the hard truth, and he also didn't want his father in on the entertainment. This one was his.

"How about next week?"

"What?" Eric seemed confused.

"The date."

"Oh. Isn't that too soon?"

"For who? I'm ready. What are you waiting for?"

"I just," he stammered. "I just started working at the base and I'm not even old enough to drink yet."

"You don't need to drink to get married." Chad pulled out his smart phone and dialed. "Hey. Set up a time and place for me to get married next week. Yeah, me. Don't worry about who, get it done and call me back with the info."

He hung up and smiled at his prey. The veiled horror on the young man's face spoke volumes. This was not part of the startup, figuring they would go this route in a year's time. Chad had his own agenda. Eventually, he would beat the name of his employer out of him. Until then, he was going to make the pretty thing suffer.

The watcher cursed under his breath as he typed in a code to signal a rise in the timeline. Every scenario had one, the people in headquarters anticipating all avenues. This was not a deal breaker, though it did put them in a bind. The young plant was to establish some connections before marrying that psychopath.

He tossed his phone on the table and continued to observe from his table in the balcony area. The guns being made for the young soldier were in the first round, and he wondered if they could be rushed. Then he remembered who the young soldier was and laughed softly. He didn't need a gun to take down Hoskins Jr. if necessary.

Even from his distance above them, he could see how the young soldier gripped the napkin in his lap with the other on the spoon. A vein rose to the surface on the back of his neck. Moments later, it receded, and the watcher breathed a sigh of relief that he could contain his anger.

In his younger years, that wasn't the case. Even battered and all bandaged up in the holding pen, the kid proved vicious. Hoskins Jr. probably thought he had the upper hand. The fact being he had no inkling who he dealt with.

The new couple finished dinner and headed outside. Following them, the watcher noticed someone else tailing them. He glimpsed him as they passed a well-lit building and knew who that man worked for; General Hoskins.

*Looks like daddy doesn't trust you, junior.*

Terrors were Hoskins' pride and joy, his own box of toys to destroy whenever he wanted. They were also expendable, which meant he needed proper soldiers as backup. An elite crew loyal to him that had expanded well past the two hundred count. They were broken into smaller groups, then sent on missions in various third world countries, in addition to the U.S. Their mission involved getting rid of the advanced troops slotted for training with the aliens.

He wasn't going to sit back and watch his people get turned into freaks for the sake of scientific discovery. Humans could defend themselves just as they were. For a long time, he had tried to iterate this to the world's military leaders, yet they wouldn't listen. They threw away their pride and now let the aliens run the show.

Then that buffoon, Perrara, always got in his way at every turn. He found out about the super soldiers being trained in the bunker, and some of his group had encountered them during a few ambushes. When a plan was called for in the states, he let his son, now a Commander, handle the logistics.

Hoskins monitored his son, the reason being his poor anger management. On more than one occasion, his son had nearly gotten a unit killed by not securing the communication channels.

Luckily, he always sent a few Terrors to cover their ass. His agenda had hit a rough patch even though he knew if he persevered, victory was at the end of the tunnel. Any way necessary to get those damned aliens off their rock.

A report from one of his men he sent to tail his son came back with the news of him marrying one of those Bi-Genetic freaks and he about flipped his shit. Because he knew his son, too stupid to not sterilize that thing before screwing it, the Hoskins bloodline would become tainted. He had seen the footage of their wedding night and shook his head in disgust.

Just as he thought, his son barely got the thing on the bed and started pumping away, getting enthralled by its scent. He heard some gargled sex talk like 'so good' and even a vulgar 'amazing pussy'. Shameful shit like that made Hoskins want to rip his son's Johnson off, it being no good anymore.

Then he thought about the little plant and knew his son was a target to get to him. Hoskins snorted. It wouldn't be that easy. Plus, he was making some leeway in cutting off Perrara's supply chains by snatching his men and torturing them until they spilled what they knew. He was sure his old pal didn't like that at all.

⌒

Vic Marzonetti found the girl pretty, Eldan begged to differ. At five feet ten, all tits and ass with lemon blonde hair, she resembled an old-time pinup made flesh. And very much Italian. He had to find some kind of outlet since Eldan refused to let him touch him. He said he couldn't have it both ways.

Either a bodyguard or nothing.

Of course, after months of unleashing his frustrations on her, she got pregnant, and they had to deal with that.

Eldan found them a hideout on the outskirts of the city after the last one got blown up by his father's crew. Four years of dodging them while establishing his name around town. The last year and a half with a baby in tow. Whenever the organization summoned Eldan, he had to lie low. That was part of the stipulation for letting them go. One had to remain in the organization as they saw fit.

The uber posh hideout used to the a former celebrity's home. His girl stretched out on the California king sized bed with their son while he did a quick check around the premises. Finding it clean, he sat down on the bed next to his new family and relaxed.

"Why does your father do this? It's so sad."

She tickled the little one as she spoke.

"He's selfish and greedy."

She sighed and caressed his cheek.

"What are you going to do now?"

"Give him a remedy."

"What do you mean?"

Vic lay down, staring at the ceiling. He didn't answer because he hadn't figured it out yet himself. There was one nagging option.

*Can I really do it?*

A few days later, Eldan returned, pulling him aside so his woman wouldn't hear.

"We do it tomorrow. In broad daylight, so they don't expect it."

Those silver eyes went blank, and Vic stepped back a bit. When they were kids, he could tell what the other thought. Now he couldn't read anything from him. Life came back into them, and he turned to him, nodding.

"Then we need a crew."

"There's about five who would stand behind me."

"Does that include me?"

"No."

"Good. I don't want anyone in my way." He looked over at the woman and child. "What about them?"

Vic held up a bottle of liquid and gently shook it at eye level.

"Good for four hours."

"You can't give that to your baby, genius."

"Then how do you suggest…"

Vic watched Eldan grab a rag, wet it with the liquid and tackle his woman on the bed. She struggled for a brief moment as he held the rag tight against her face. When she lay still, he reached for something out of his inside jacket pocket. He held an eyedropper with a dark liquid and squeezed its contents into the baby's mouth. His son cried out, obviously from the taste, and then went still.

"Let's go."

Eldan got up from the bed and headed for the door. When Vic didn't follow, he turned towards him. He stood staring at him with a new kind of fear. He finally figured out what the organization had turned him into.

A Monster.

With a seven-man team, they arrived on the edge of the Marzonetti homestead. A few thugs positioned around the front left the back under-manned. Splitting into three groups, they circled around and got close enough to see inside the house. The one thing he hated about the way his father ran the family was the lackluster security. That was how his abduction happened. His crew went in without announcement and began the assault on the Marzonetti palace.

He beat down two men who came at him shooting by dodging the bullets. Ahead of him, Eldan appeared to walk leisurely as he tossed bodies on either side of him. They made a pathway to his father's office where his loyal men protected him. All four were present when Vic kicked open the door.

"I'm home," he said. "Father."

Eldan easily dispatched the men coming at. Vic grabbed the gun from the man next to him falling dead to the floor and aimed. His father jumped from out of his seat, gun in hand, and Vic pulled the trigger, putting multiple holes in the man's front side. His body twitched and twisted with each hit until he fell back into the chair, a bloody mess of swiss cheese. As he turned to the door, he grabbed the fallen gun and shot his father's men in the back of the head.

"Now my reign begins."

A silver ring of light glowed in Vic Marzonetti's eyes as he looked down in hatred at the bodies.

The cell door opened, letting the hall lights beam through the tiny space. All the prisoner could see was a dark silhouette, not their features. He was too tired to move and waited for whatever would come next. He had been beaten, tortured, and trained like nothing he had experienced before. Haggard and wearing dingy clothes, he hadn't eaten in three days. Every time they brought him back to his cell, chains were attached to keep him anchored to the wall. As if he had the strength to escape after all that was done to him.

*Maybe they've come to finish me off.*

"When we snatched you up along with the Marzonetti kid, we knew you would come in handy." The surprisingly smooth male voice said.

He squinted to try getting a glimpse of his captor. From what he could decipher, the man wore a uniform of sorts. Light glinted off the shine of his shoes.

"Working for the old Don was a waste of your talent.

We've made you much stronger over these past years, so you can do your job properly."

"And what job is that?"

"Time to resume your duty at house Marzonetti."

Back in a nice suit and feeling clean, the bodyguard Bartoni, straightened the sleeves of his jacket and stared off in the distance. The desert air smelled arid, and he longed for water. Ahead of him was the transport that would take him home. In addition, was a large cargo with the Marzonetti insignia on it. The coordinator came to stand beside him.

"What's in the box," he asked the man.

"A gift for the Marzonetti inner circle." Bartoni made a face. "Don't worry, you'll like it." The coordinator turned and headed back into the bunker. "Safe journey. And remember our agreement."

"Yeah, I'm sure you won't let me forget." He scratched his forearm where a fresh tattoo of the Marzonetti crest lay and stopped himself. Letting out a loud sigh, he got into the transport. "Let's see what home is like."

When his transport delivered him to the front of the Marzonetti homestead, he didn't see much difference at first. As he got closer, it became obvious what the change was. He didn't recognize most of the men around the perimeter, and many of them looked petrified. Two men came running up to him.

"State your business or you die right here!"

He grabbed the barrel of the rifle and swung the man into his partner. They went sideways into the grass on top of each other. More guns aimed at him, and his eyes did a rapid scan of their positions.

"Stand down!"

The voice came from the balcony. He looked up into

the spitting image of his old boss as a young Don. He recognized Vic instantly. And his former charge seemed to remember him as well.

"Now tell me how it is you show up out of the blue after all this time?"

"Same to you," Bartoni replied.

Vic Marzonetti frowned and gripped the edge of the stone balcony.

"I see you learned a few things while you were away."

"Not by choice."

"It never is with those people."

A van came up the driveway, circled around and backed in towards the front entrance.

"A gift for the family."

"We can unpack that later. Come inside."

He saw damage being repaired and had a flashback of the abduction. Some of the debris appeared to be months old.

"What happened here? Where's your father?"

Vic sat down in a new chair in his father's office and placed his legs across the desk.

"Dead."

"How? Was there a raid?"

He smiled.

"I killed that narcissistic fucker."

Bartoni's eyes narrowed as he took it all in. Everything the coordinator told him turned out to be true then. Movement out of the corner of his eye made him jump and his gaze met a white-haired man. The silver eyes gave away his identity.

That kid too?

"So," the new Don said. "Why were you sent back?"

"To head up your security detail. And not a moment too soon, cuz it's shit."

Six men hauled the giant crate into the foyer and set

it down in clear line of sight of the office.

Vic pointed to it.

"No idea." He found the crowbar attached to the side and pulled it off. "Shall we?"

"Just because it has our family crest on it doesn't mean it won't blow up and kill us all."

"Oh," Bartoni said. "They have no intention of getting rid of you anytime soon."

He broke the seal on the crate with the help of two other men and lifted the top off. Inside were guns. Not just any guns, either. They were beautifully crafted black lacquered gunmetal and silver, with the Mazonetti crest on them.

Vic, Eldan, and he stood staring down in awe over the crate. He picked it up a small box with his name on it. Opening it, he breathed in hard.

The gun inside was nearly identical to the others, except the family insignia was a deep red on both sides of the handle. A note lay on the bottom, along with boxes of rounds.

Protect the Marzonetti family honor.

He looked over at Vic, also reading the note.

"Welcome to a new era for our family," Vic announced.

# Four : The Elite

## FALL OF A GENERAL

The Impaler presently only got called out whenever the organization required extreme torture to get vital information. Your average run-of-the-mill torture package included breaking of limbs, removal of body parts, etcetera. His kind involved something different.

Most of the time, the victim begged for a limb or two to be broken instead. Word had gotten around, and he had become famous in the underworld.

A small unit of four agents stood around the chair they had tied the subject to. They had already beaten him up a bit, and he still refused to tell them what they wanted to hear. A single light bulb shined down on him from above. He wore a shit-eating grin on his face as if he had won.

An agent pulled out a cigarette case from his shirt's breast pocket and took one out. He slowly stuck it in the corner of his mouth and lit it with a beautifully carved silver lighter. After a few puffs, he took the cigarette from his mouth and stared down at the man.

"The Impaler will be here shortly."

The man stiffened, his face seeming to melt as it drooped down in despair.

"You're lying! Just trying to get me to talk. I ain't telling you people nothing!"

"Mmm. Yes, you've said that. So, we called The Impaler."

"Bring it on, you sacks of shit. He won't get me to

say anything either." He gave a nervous laugh. "You're going to have to kill me and then you'll have to start all over from scratch."

The bay door opened and Dr. Winston Sterling, wearing a casual suit, strolled in carrying a cloth case.

"Then, if that's what must be done, I can make this quick," he said.

Another agent pulled a small table from the other side of the room and set it by the victim. The doctor placed his roll up bag on it and stretched his arms upwards. Then he undid the straps that held the bundle together and rolled it open flat.

Gleaming metal rods of different size gauges displayed neatly in a row commanded attention. He pulled one of the small ones out and the light caught its detail. What appeared to be a solid straight rod actually had tiny threads winding along its length. Sections where the twists connect glinted like diamonds.

The victim sucked in air through his teeth and tried to back farther into the chair.

"You think sticking me with one of your fancy needles is going to make me talk?"

"I thought we already established that you would have to die." The doctor inspected the rod, turning it side to side. "This will be quite painful for you." He motioned to the agents.

They strapped the victim down tighter around his wrists, ankles, and neck. He tried to struggle against being tethered to where he could barely move an inch. The doctor leaned over him and planted a hand on the victim's shoulder, feeling for something.

"Hmm. Let's start here."

He positioned the rod at an odd angle above the skin where his finger was and pushed. Slowly. The victim gritted his teeth at first, his leg jumping without the ability of full motion, then he screamed. The rod had only gone a quarter of the way in and the Impaler continued to insert it. Slowly. Tears and snot oozed from the victim's face as his voice tapered out, becoming hoarse. With the rod completely in, two inches were exposed on each end.

The Impaler stood back to admire his work.

"Not bad. I found that pressure point fairly quick."

He perused his assortment of rods and picked out another small gauge one. This time, he felt around the victim's side near the kidney. The victim's eyes widened, and he squirmed to no avail. Positioning the rod at the insertion point above his finger, the Impaler once again went with slow precision.

The agents endured the unbearable screaming. That part they all hated, having said as much when alone together. They didn't dare say anything to The Impaler. When the victim's body convulsed, they all looked away. It would stop soon because that monster would tap another pressure point linked to it. Sure enough, he did, and the victim looked worse for wear.

A smell lingered, and they realized the victim had shit his shorts. That never seemed to deter The Impaler. He found an even smaller gauge and lifted it high in the air before turning back to the victim. Something in his eyes changed. A coldness that left them all rooted where they stood.

In a flash, he had the victim's head held with one hand and the other positioned the rod right in the inner corner of his left eye. His mouth curved into an inhuman smile, teeth exposed, as he brought the rod closer.

The agent closest to the chair clamped a hand over his own mouth to stop himself from vomiting. Another agent standing on the opposite side of the table got a perfect view and too horrified to look away.

The rod went in.

The victim found enough in him to scream even more. His body went stiff while the man kept his eyelid open as he enjoyed his work. With the rod placed like the others, one end protruding out the back of his head, The Impaler let out a loud sigh and stood back up.

"Well, what do you think?" He asked. The victim's mouth moved. "What was that?"

"I…I'll talk," the victim whispered again.

"Is that so?" He turned to the agents. "Pity. I guess you don't need me, then?"

"No," the first agent barely got out before he spewed vomit along the floor by his feet.

The Impaler went to remove the first rod and the other agent blocked his hand.

"Sorry, could you wait until he tells us what we need to know?"

"Of course." The Impaler stepped away and waited by the bay door, not listening to any of the information transpiring.

When they finished interrogating the victim, the second agent summoned him over with a wave. He took hold of the first rod.

"This will hurt even more," he hissed with elation.

Pulling the rods straight out would rip apart the tissue, leaving a gaping shredded wound. They had to be removed in the same way they were inserted; slowly with rotation.

All four agents moved away, not bearing to watch the man gleefully untwist the rods out of their victim, who continued to scream until he thankfully passed out.

After extracting his rods, The Impaler cleaned them with a solution he sprayed then patted dry with a soft cloth. He stowed them back in the bag and rolled it up, securing the straps again. Slinging it over his shoulder, he exited the safe house.

Outside, his work phone dinged. He checked the message.

Major multiple car accident. Mass incoming.

*Time to play doctor again.*

He popped the trunk of his car and threw the bag in. Slamming it shut, he got in the driver's seat and pushed the start button. There he pondered which job he hated more.

~

A tidal wave of apple juice splashed in Erica's face and soaked the front of Erica's top. The now empty cup bounced off and landed on the kitchen floor. Her daughter's face wrinkled with hate, her eyes burning with indignation.

"I said, I wanted milk with my pancakes!"

At twelve years old, the girl was a monster. Daddy's little girl. Her twin brother sat uncomfortable silence beside her. The next oldest, her fifteen-year-old son, didn't bother to look up from his breakfast, visibly upset. She stared into empty space, not acknowledging her daughter's rant.

Nearly twenty years had passed since she married her husband, now a General like his father. Their wedding night etched in her soul. She shuddered, at how he stripped her naked before they even got to the bedroom.

He held her down by her neck while he plowed his cock into her like an angry animal. Praising how good it was through his grunting. He claimed her as his own piece of property to do with as he pleased and those were the better days.

Since the demise of his father's status, the former General, he had become obsessed with the old man's agenda. That also meant he took his frustrations out on her at every turn.

Their oldest daughter had joined the Navy right out of high school and deployed at nineteen on a ship somewhere. She had literally fled the house. Her younger brother, less than a year apart in age, did the same this past year. The animosity within the house walls was more than they could take.

"Don't you ignore me!" Her daughter screamed.

"Stop it!"

Her twin brother slammed his cup on the table.

She went to the refrigerator, got out the milk, and poured some in a glass. Her daughter reached over and snatched it from her before she filled it, spilling milk that mingled with the apple juice. Satisfied, she continued to eat the peach and blueberry pancakes on the plate in front of her. Her favorite, which she demanded often.

"Hurry up and finish. The car will be here soon to take you all to school."

The girl shoved a whole pancake in her mouth and chewed like a cow, locking eyes with her while she did it, knowing how uncivilized she looked. And that she hated that. She reached over to take the fifteen-year-old's cup and he smacked her hand away.

"I know how to take care of my own dishes," he snapped.

This resulted from their father treating them like gold in defiance of her discipline. A battle she decided early on not to fight, yet her husband pushed her into every time. The sound of the front door opening made her tense up.

General Chad Hoskins walked into the kitchen. Seeing the mess on the floor, his face flushed pink. He glared at her. It didn't matter whose fault. She would be punished for it.

"What the fuck is all this?"

"I was just about to clean it up."

"All this time and you still don't know how to not

make a goddamn mess?"

"That's right, Daddy. She's such a slob."

A slight grin tugged at the corners of his mouth. They were a tag team when it came to ganging up on her. Their daughter's eyes twinkled as she shoved another pancake in her mouth, her legs swinging back and forth under the table.

A car horn blowing made them all perk up.

"Let's go," Hoskins ordered.

"I'm not done yet," their daughter said.

He leaned over the table so that his face was mere inches from hers. She looked up and reared back in fright.

"I said, let's go."

"Okay."

Her husband stood up and said in her ear.

"I'll deal with you later."

The four of them left the kitchen and she sighed in relief. She cleaned up then went into the bedroom to take off the now sticky clothes. In the bathroom, she wiped herself off. As she walked into her closet, she tapped a hidden space on the wall. Panels flipped open along the walls while she got her uniform out. Shifting back into male form, the once young soldier went to a glass box with red velvet lining. Inside were two guns, the metal a dark chocolate color with the organization symbol in dark blue to create a subtle contrast.

He liked his promotion at the base to a field officer because it got him out of the office away from the General. It was also convenient to do jobs for the organization whenever they arose. Taking only one gun, he stowed it in the holster and straightened out his uniform.

Not even an hour after arriving, an agent called him into a supply closet to relay an order.

The timeframe; eight minutes. If done right, he would be back at the office and none the wiser. After memorizing the location, he hurried out the back way. As the door closed, he spotted his husband rounding the corner towards his office.

He took off his uniform jacket, shoved it in the small hiding place he had in a crack on the side of the building, then headed down the alleyway. It took ten minutes double timing it to the site, and he still had to climb up iron bar steps to the roof. A large briefcase sat against the edge.

Opening the case, he found the dismantled sniper rifle and one round. That was all he needed. Once he reassembled the rifle and locked on the target, he waited. The counter went down in seconds and minutes. Through the lens, he saw two people enter the room of the building across from him.

The smaller of the two appeared to struggle with the other. Battered and bloody, the poor kid was no match. As the man dropped him onto the floor and grabbed a pair of handcuffs lying on the counter, he pulled the trigger.

The man's head exploded like a busted watermelon, brain matter making a pattern on the wall. On the floor, the little boy was screaming. He didn't have to hear it to know. Dismantling and packing up the rifle, he saw agents burst into the room and retrieve the boy. The counter displayed two minutes left.

༄

White as pure snow, the tall, slender man walked among the crowded commuters on the sidewalk. Dressed nearly all in white: the shirt with carnation pink tie, shoes, pants, vest and full-length coat. He seemed invisible, somehow not brushed against or forced to stop for others. Platinum blonde hair cascaded down his back under the white wide-brimmed hat.

No one acknowledged his presence, yet the crowd seemed to flow around him.

Even when his hand produced a short sword with a carved bone white handle and cut down the man ahead of him, not a soul noticed. Blood flew everywhere except on him. Not a drop touched him. He continued to walk at the same pace, sheathing his sword. Perfect pink lips formed a tiny smile.

The man walking next to the victim froze in place. Looking around, desperate to find out what happened, he saw a blur of white before it disappeared. He hurried forward into the nearest building's doorway, shivering. Then the screaming started. People parted like the red sea as blood spread across the sidewalk.

The Snowman lurked in the city.

He pulled his phone from his pants pocket and dialed the boss' number. When no one answer, he sent a text and received one promptly back for a nearby safe house nearby. Careful to avoid the police, he made a bee-line for the location. He burst into the little apartment and went straight for the bar.

"What happened?" One of his colleagues shouted.

"I saw him," he replied shakily.

"Saw who?" The third man in the room asked.

"Snowman. I saw the Snowman."

He took a giant swig of whiskey from the bottle.

"That's impossible. If you did, you'd be dead."

"Yeah, no one's ever lived to tell," the first guy said.

"I know what I saw!" he yelled.

He slammed the bottle down.

"Do you?"

The other male voice didn't come from any of them, and they all turned towards whoever spoke. Sitting on the island, one leg stretched out, the other bended with an arm resting on the knee, the man in white raised his head. The light caught his silver eyes.

"Oh, God!" The victim's friend cried out.

A breeze ruffled his hair, making him go rigid. His eyes fell on the blade, dripping blood, running off clean. He heard thuds behind him and knew his colleagues were dead.

"Please," he whispered.

The Snowman came out of his stance and stood straight. In a flash, he came within inches of the man's face, his gaze unwavering.

"You'll send your boss a message for me, won't you?"

The man nodded his head. He had no other choice.

～

Professor Morandi gave up on her favorite assistant long ago. Kevin accepted that fact, immersing himself in the organization's work. Finding it more his calling than he had imagined. He didn't blame the upper levels for keeping him on a leash. Let loose on his own, he indiscriminately killed. The way he had tortured that General who invaded Morandi's facility should have been his clue.

Dressed in a light grey suit with a deep blue shirt, he walked right into the bank and shot both guards, the teller, and the manager who ran for the alarm. That done, he ripped the cameras off the walls and headed for the safe. A guerilla unit opposing human intervention used the bank as a front to fund a coup.

Did they not know their actions went against human interest? He took a deep breath. Raising his hands in front of him, he focused his power into a bright light that shot out and melted a hole big enough for him to walk through.

There wasn't much in terms of money, maybe about forty million. The weapons were the genuine treasure. He scoured through the room and found a box with an interesting logo on it.

*Bingo!* He tapped his earbud.

"All yours."

A scurry to his left from behind had him barely dodging a dagger that swiped across his vision. Smiling, he caught the culprit by the arm and swung him into the wall. When that didn't deter the man, he slammed his foot into his abdomen. With a firm grip, he pulled the man's arm right out of its socket. The whole time, he laughed maniacally. The man's screams only lasted a few seconds as Kevin snapped his neck.

Disgusted at the splotches of blood on his beautiful suit, he kicked the man's face in until it resembled stewed tomatoes and walked out of the bank. He shielded his eyes from the glaring sun with one hand as he got into his car.

When the lab analyzed his DNA, it showed markers of Senigranke. A race of predators who could evolve into what were called Litigators. Rare beings capable of manipulating a planet's axis. As a hybrid human, that talent appeared dormant while his other powers manifested. The female alien had worked with him to hone most of it, and she encouraged him to do what he felt, even if it meant killing.

He checked his hair in the rearview mirror. Small flecks were visible in his blonde strands. Unacceptable. An urge to go back in and dismantle the man surged. Then he saw the agents show up and squelched it. He shouldn't still be in the area, so drove off quickly, hoping they hadn't spotted him earlier. On the dash touchscreen, he saw a message from home.

Home.

He never thought about soemthing like family after his teen years. Professor Morandi saw herself as a maternal figure, except she had lust in her eyes every time they were together. Not very motherly in his book. Now he had children. Four of them who kept him on his toes every day. Morandi would not have approved.

At the hidden house deep on the outskirts of the city, he pulled into the garage that sloped down, ending farther underground to get to its main level. He had built it on a hillside to make sure it could only be visible from the shoreline on the other side. The organization felt it necessary, considering his job. Many enemies knew what he looked like because early on he didn't care. If any of them went after his children, the city would rain in blood.

Inside, he hurried out of the car and ran two steps at a time up to the bathroom. He stripped off all his clothes and got in the tub. Turning the shower on as hot as he could stand it, he scrubbed himself clean with a bar of soap. No matter the amount of body washes on the market, a well-made bar bested them for cleaning the body.

Laughter and running came to his ears over the sound of the rushing water, and he sighed. He turned off the shower and stepped out, scooping up the bloody clothes and shoving them in the lower compartment of the sink for now.

His children came bursting into the bathroom.

"Daddy!" they yelled together with arms outstretched.

His daughter halted and skidded back.

"Eww! Dad!"

His oldest son also backed off and slapped a hand over his eyes.

"Clothes, Dad! Clothes!"

The younger ones couldn't care less about him being naked and slammed into him.

"What did you expect, charging into my bathroom?"

"We missed you, Daddy!" The two clinging to him chimed up.

He bent down and gave them a hug. His daughter turned her back to him.

"So, how was your trip?"

"Uneventful. Went all that way and it only took less than an hour."

"Well," his oldest said. "At least you're getting paid."

"There is that." He got the little ones to disengage. "Okay, everybody out."

When they were gone, he stood in front of the sink and leaned on it with both hands. Sometimes he wished for their mother. An enemy had found out about her three years ago and killed her, making it look like an accident to the normal bystander.

He knew immediately what had happened, as did the organization. No one could stop him from hunting the man down and tearing him apart. He sent the pieces to his faction's main hideout as a message.

⌣

Swirls of light danced in front of his eyes as Damon heard the cryochamber depressurize. The loud hissing assaulted his ears. He felt the ice melting on his skin and attempted to move his still stiff body. And the pain; so much pain. They had put him in cryo for the third time and more times than he wanted to remember in the regeneration chamber.

Being a police detective was bad enough. Going above and beyond his duties for the organization had him wishing for death many times.

Different assignments to precincts in multiple cities around the Americas, staying for only a few years at a time, became part of his life.

New rules and regulations within law enforcement included all kinds of authorized prototype weapons. Great for the side of good, but also a curse. Criminals loved new toys to try out on them.

A technician came to lean over him with a pained smile on his face.

"How are we doing this time?"

His lungs felt like they were swimming in liquid, and it hurt when he tried to make a sound. The technician saw him struggle and left, coming back with an eyedropper. He squeezed the liquid down his throat and Damon felt the warmth course his esophagus. Clearing his throat, he answered.

"Hurt."

"Yeah, this was bad. We had a time keeping you alive. You kept slipping away."

"How long?"

"A few years. Five."

"Shit!"

Despite it hurting like hell, he clenched his hands into fists. The only thing he could do to show his frustration. He hated missing years like that. The last time he lost three years and technology had made another leap when he came out. His vision cleared up enough to see the medical wing had changed slightly. It was still mostly white, with a few splashes of color visible.

"Let's get you up."

The technician slid a hand underneath behind his back and lifted him upright. Damon winced as his bones and muscles protested. Great. He would be in rehab again for about six months before being thrown back into the fray.

"I think you'll be pleased to know that not much has changed this time. Everything seems to be at a standstill with the cold hard truth of war getting closer."

"Everyone's just now figuring that out?"

Another technician came over and draped a robe around his shoulders before forcing his arms into the sleeves. He endured his limbs as they screamed in agony. The Technician placed a small hard coated chewable in his mouth and the fruity flavor surprised him as he waited for the usual nastiness.

"Oh, we fixed that, though."

"Took you long enough," he muttered.

That sensation of euphoria enveloped him, and his body relaxed. The pain subsided. A beep indicated the chamber venting had competed. It lowered, giving him time to prepare for the real test. He swung his legs over when the chamber base got low enough for his feet to touch the cold tiled floor, then went to stand. Lucky for him, the two technicians were near and caught him when his legs buckled.

"Get the chair," the first one ordered one of the staff.

"I don't need!" He fell back on the chamber bed and gripped the edge to try again.

"How about we not do the whole invincible bit and let us help you?"

"I don't…"

Damon felt the tears, which made him angrier.

He saw the technician nod at someone behind him and knew what came next. With no way to defend himself, he felt the needle enter his skin. Irrational fear of going back to sleep gripped him and he couldn't help being paranoid. The room blurred, then it was lights out.

Damon bolted upright and found himself on the bed of his temporary quarters in the bunker. Sparse in furniture and personal items, it suited him fine. All metal, grey and white contemporary occupied the space. He glanced at the digital time display and saw the date.

Five years.

He still couldn't believe it. A sharp headache hit him and he saw flashes of his last memory.

*Fuck that noise.*

Throwing the covers off, he went to stand and fell to the floor. His hands caught the edge of the bed and he pulled himself back up. He cursed at his fragility and laid there panting. Beads of sweat had formed all over and he wondered if he was indeed sick. It had happened the first time he came out of cryo.

His door opened to let in the therapist. He took one look at Damon sprawled on the bed and shook his head.

"Why do you always push harder than you need to? We have all the time in the world."

"Really? Tell that to the aliens trying to wipe us out in the near future."

"I'm getting the chair." The therapist walked out.

Damon punched the bed and buried his face in the blanket. Already in his mid-forties, he looked like he hadn't aged a day since his training days.

*How long are they going to keep doing this to me?*

Physical therapy only lasted four months this time. He readied himself to get the hell out of the bunker. Not too thrilled to return to police work, there had to be some compromise. The transport dropped him off at an old loft apartment building. His new home, compared to the one at the bunker, classified as a dump. A studio with dim sunlight coming through, accenting the dark, dusty space. He kind of liked the aesthetic because it conveyed his soul at that moment.

He set down his meager belongings and plopped down on the bed, stretching out his body. The bed easily held his six-foot four frame, which counted as a plus. A strange tone emitted from his coat pocket, and he dug in to retrieve the culprit. The newest commlink made to look like a smart phone.

*Did technology go backwards?*

The message on the screen showed where he was to report and what his duties were. He grimaced. The same as when he left: same city, different area. He scrolled down and saw the attachment. Clicking it open, he sat up and gripped the phone tight. His face scrunched up and his body quaked.

*Not this. No more.*

Defeated, he hit the home screen and got out of bed.

*Time to meet my fate.*

The precinct looked like all the others, except this time, his desk sat farther in the back. He walked in, went past the row of desks on the upper platform, then down the twelve steps to the main office floor. To the left at the bottom he saw a desk with everything arranged neatly. He shook his head as he made the turn and continued to the back.

Before the row ended, he turned right and there, along the wall, were three large desks. The one in the middle had his name plaque. There were five desks across from the three.

At the second desk of the five were two detectives who stood staring at him intently. They had the air of being corrupt and not giving a damn who knew it. Damon pinched the bridge of his nose and winced in exasperation.

*Again?*

"Hey, big shot," the blonde one called out. "Think you got more clout when it comes to drug busts, don't ya'?"

Damon sat in his chair and put his feet up on his desk. "Nope."

"Let me tell you something," the other piped in. "I don't care how seasoned you are, in here you're a newbie and it's in your best interest to follow our lead."

Someone snorted, and another male detective laughed.

"Follow their lead and you may end up getting reamed by internal affairs."

The one who laughed came up to his desk and held out a hand.

"Detective Paulson."

Damon shook his hand.

"Nice to meet you."

"Don't worry about those two hard asses."

"Hey!" The blonde one yelled. "Fuck you, Paulson."

"Enough!"

Everyone on the floor stopped what they were doing and turned to that voice.

The captain stood in the middle with a disgusted look on his face. He scanned the room, daring any of them to say something. When no one did, he pointed to Damon.

"You! In my office, now."

Damon swung his legs off the desk and followed the captain. Inside the office, he found it refreshing. Simple décor and file cabinets lined the walls. His new dossier lay in the desk with more underneath.

"I swear, every place you go to this happens. Look," the captain folded his hands and rested his chin on them. "I've been sworn to keep this all under wraps, but you have to at least try and get along with my guys if we're going to stop this thing."

"I didn't start it," Damon answered defensively.

"You never do. I don't like the government meddling in my cases, but with aliens doing all kinds of crazy shit, we need all the help we can get."

"Right."

"Get out of my office." As he opened the door, the captain added, "and stay out of trouble. I have assigned you a partner per your superior's instructions."

A uniformed officer now occupied the desk by the steps. The name tag said Lt. Nathan Inslee. Young, kind of chubby in the face, and sandy blonde hair. Cute. Then he pulled a clear plastic takeout container from a brown bag and set it on the desk. Damon cringed. The different shades of green mixed with slithers of orange and black made him gag. Salad. Before the officer could pop that thing open, he advanced on him.

"Hey, let's go for some Chinese."

Officer Inslee reared back, startled. Then his eyes narrowed.

"You're the new detective I have to drive around."

"That's a roger."

"We don't go driving around unless there's a case."

"But, I'm starving." He gave a wide smile.

"So am I," Inslee snapped.

"Then why are you about to eat that? It's not real food."

Inslee's face turned bright pink, and others in the room snickered.

"I'm on a diet," he replied softly.

Damon rolled his eyes. Grabbing the officer by the wrist, he hauled him up and headed towards the door.

"If we're going to be riding together, we should get to know each other better. First things first. Food is life."

Inslee tried to get away unsuccessfully. Damon was on a mission.


All the businesses on the block were in full swing, the weather being mild that day. Foot traffic crowded the sidewalk, it not being noon yet. They two officers had just eaten breakfast not two hours ago. Damon covered his eyes to block out the sunlight as he exited the donut shop and slid into the passenger side of the squad car parked in front.

His partner's horrified expression when he came out with the red and white paper basket of gooey goodness. Priceless. He stuck one of the churro donuts covered in Bavarian cream with the wooden pick and raised it to Inslee's mouth.

"Say ahh," he laughed.

"Stop it!"

"Come on," he chided as he moved it around in a circle. "At least take a bite."

"No. I don't want any." A plastic container filled to the brim with salad, no meat anywhere in sight sat beside him. Not even cheese.

"Yes, you do."

Right as Inslee opened his mouth to say something, Damon shoved it in. He gave the dirtiest look yet as he chewed. Which made Damon burst out laughing.

The radio crackled, interrupting their game, and the dashboard's touch screen lit up. Multiple frantic voices came through from different channels. Codes went flying amidst the yelling.

Robbery in progress. Suspects fleeing the scene. Assailants are armed and dangerous. Officers down. In pursuit of suspects. Barricade broken through. More officers down.

A new voice cut through on a secure channel. It silenced the others.

"Detective Peterson, I need you to rendezvous at these coordinates and assist with detainment of the suspects." Numbers flashed on the dashboard screen.

"Really?" Damon snorted.

"If we cannot apprehend them, then phase two will be in effect."

The message ended as the last of the donuts disappeared into his mouth.

"Let's go," he said.

"That's out of our jurisdiction. Why would they call you out to it?"

"Drive. And don't get out of this vehicle for any reason."

"What?"

Damon looked over at him, and Inslee flinched.

"Fine. We're going."

It took ten minutes to get to the next barricade set up along a busy street. They had evacuated most of the people from the area. Onlookers were still there with cell phones raised to capture the action.

"Go past and park around the corner."

The moment the car stopped, Damon hopped out and headed towards the officers lying in wait. He stood next to the commanding officer. The man's face flushed pink with anger, and he yelled out orders with a bullhorn to make the barricade of squad cars tighter.

"What's the status so far?"

"Fuckers killed three of ours already at the scene. They rammed right through the barricade a mile out and took a few more with them. Got eight men down in critical." He paused. "Ran down a bunch of pedestrians, too. Children even."

"And now?"

"Nothing seems to stop them."

"Humans?"

The commanding officer turned to him; his face contorted in disgust.

"Unfortunately, yeah."

Wheels squealing off in the distance made them look up. An older four-door model sedan fishtailed around the corner and came barreling down the deserted road. Damon's vision zeroed in on the passengers. He could see their bloodlust plain as day.

*Detainment? Fuck that!*

Another vehicle came screechinig to an angled stop

beside the commander's car as Damon whipped off his coat and walked over. The driver got out and handed him a long bundle in black cloth. He took it and drew out a black lacquered scabbard with intricate silver designs carved in it.

Damon unsheathed the sword, its blade gleaming cold in the sunlight. Nearly the same height as him and equally heavy, he was used to wielding it over the years.

The suspects got closer, never letting up speed, and Damon knew they would break through again. He could see the front grill had been modified to withstand high impact and the vehicle itself was probably weighed down for stability.

The officers behind the squad cars opened fire, some getting hit in return by the suspects in the back seat. Lots of yelling ensued, as the officers tried to grab the wounded and get out of the way as the car smashed through, flipping over the two in front. They went sprawling in different directions, landing on others nearby.

Loud laughter, profanity and boasting came from the suspects' vehicle.

"Playtime is over," Damon said, more to himself than them.

He positioned himself near their line of sight and went into a defense stance, blade pointed behind him over his right shoulder. The driver made eye contact and smiled viciously. The roar of the engine let Damon know he had stepped down on the accelerator. It headed straight for him. At the last moment, he took a sidestep and brought forth the blade so that it spanned across the entire front of the vehicle.

It went through the sedan like sliced bread, the vehicle's speed giving it ease of travel. He saw the glow of his eyes reflected in the windshield as the sword glided seamlessly, slicing everything in half as the car passed him. The suspects didn't know what was happening until it was too late.

The vehicle came apart midair, spraying blood and fluids onto the pavement before bursting into flames. It landed near a crowd of people who, against their better judgment, were filming too close. They ran screaming for cover, some of them not making it in time. Debris flew everywhere.

Damon stood in the middle of the street, sword in hand. Not a drop of blood on it. The man ran over to him and he handed it over. The sword went back into its sheath and wrapped in the cloth bag. Seconds later, the man drove off.

"What the fuck?" A reporter asked. "Has it got so damn bad that we need policemen with swords now?"

"This is bullshit," another detective shouted.

"They killed our brethren! Justice was done," another officer retorted.

"Not like this!"

A shop owner stepped onto the sidewalk and stared at Damon, his eyes bulging. The commanding officer appeared shell-shocked. Those in the crowd who came out unscathed continued their live feeds, commenting in raised voices.

"Well, I guess this has gone viral by now," the commanding officer finally spoke. "Get the hell out of here before any more hell breaks loose."

As he turned to leave, Damon caught sight of Inslee in the squad car, head turned towards the road, awestruck.

*Damn it!*

He didn't want his partner to see that.

Don Vic Marzonetti lounged on the giant chair he had an interior designer make in an empty banquet hall he converted to a private lounge area. Two sofas faced each other before him with velvety dark red carpet underneath.

On one of them Eldan slumped, half asleep as usual. The man could hear a pin drop. That alone he found frightening. He wore the short dark-haired wig and contacts that made his eyes blue. A sheathed sword with a black lacquered handle stood ropped up by his side.

Bartoni stood to his right carrying the gun gifted to the family by the organization in a shoulder holster. When he returned after so many years, like he did, Vic remained suspicious at first. The organization had too many things up their sleeves.

He still didn't like the fact that he had to deal with them, knowing what was really going on and couldn't blame them. Humans had all but given over the reins to their governments and went about business as usual, not thinking about the impending doom. In addition to his family, he noticed some of the other major crime families with similar guns. The organization had essentially branded everyone involved.

His children, now totaling five, got tangled up in it as well. His oldest son had branched off on his own renown around the city as a monster. The next to the youngest, Anais, worked at a private resort run by the biggest crime family in three countries. Thankfully, the other three just indulged in whatever perks they could get, being Marzonettis, his daughter especially.

"We seem to have a visitor," Bartoni said, as his hand fell from his ear.

"This late in the day? Who is it?"

Bartoni pointed ahead, and Vic frowned.

His familiar FBI agent waltzed through like he owned

the place, a crooked grin on his face.

"Don Marzonetti! How's it going? Kill anyone lately?"

"Thinking about it," he replied, eyeing the agent.

"Sure about that?" He stood in the middle of the lounge area with one hand in his pocket. "Cause we got some dead mafia flunkies floating in the river uptown."

"That's got nothing to do with our family," his head of security said.

The agent turned and gave him a nasty look.

"It all has to do with your family," he spat.

Vic leaned forward in his chair.

"My family is not the only one in this area."

"No, but your family's reputation precedes you."

"That was then. I don't run things like that."

The agent snorted in disgust.

"None of you will ever change. You're all scum."

The sound of a sword unsheathing got their attention, making the agent's eyes wider. Even with baby blue eyes, Eldan oozed malice. Neither man noticed he had stood in a relaxed stance, sword lowered, ready to strike.

"You should reevaluate where you are right now."

"Is your fucking butler threatening me?"

"No one would miss you," Eldan continued as he raised the sword.

"I think it's time for you to leave," Bartoni said.

Scared and angry, the agent turned on his heels and fled the room.

"Stupid bastard," Bartoni laughed.

"Are those bodies…" Vic asked.

"Nope." Then his head cocked to one side. "Maybe one or two?"

Vic hung his head and huffed. He turned to Eldan sheathing his sword. The killer shook his head.

"Find out what's going on. If someone is marking bodies with our signature, I want their head on a stick."

He watched Bartoni walk out to do his bidding. "I don't like government agents paying me visits every month."

The watcher perched in the trees across from the Marzonetti property waited for Bartoni to leave the homestead before climbing down. He knew exactly where the bodies came from and shook his head at HQ, letting a sloppy job like that go forward.

Meant to start a small war between two top mafia families, it oviously didn't go well. And the two thrown in from a separate incident just looked bad. Every move a chess piece, like the calculations in a game of shogi. Depending on how they pushed, determined who would be left standing in the end.

For his money, he bet on the Marzonettis.

⌒

General Hoskins drank his coffee black, no sugar, and very particular about where it came from. So, when his assistant explained they were out of his usual brand and the one in the mug could be just as good, he tossed it in the young soldier's face.

Screaming ensued and other soldiers invaded his office, rushing to see what was wrong. They summoned a Corman to help haul the soldier off to medical.

He had been irritated all week because of some troubling information he received. Some of his smaller guerilla units were either wiped out or exposed, with bad timing. Only one explanation: a mole. His father's actions behind the scenes no longer a secret, they figured with him out if the picture, no one remained to carry out his agenda.

Thinking back to all the times he made calls, some of them were inside the house. He had established long ago his wife may be some sort of spy and at present couldn't pinpoint who she worked for. A few years ago, he thought maybe he had been wrong about her, then she would do something out of character.

One day, whiile on the ladder fixing something, she dropped the hammer. Her reflexes were lightning fast and her stability on the ladder as she arched back to catch it was on par with the best soldiers he had seen. Yet, she acted like a sort of klutz around the house.

He made a note to check his home office for bugs again, even though the last sweep found nothing. If not in there, then somewhere in the house. His private commlink made a soft blip, and he opened his desk drawer to see what it said.

Bravo location leaked. Direct tie to you.

Extraction suggested.

Hoskins slammed his fist on the desk, creating a loud bang that made everyone outside his office look over. He stood up and walked to the doorway. His wife, in male form somewhere in the building, wouldn't be done with his meeting for a while. He grabbed his hat off the top of the coat rack and headed out.

Time to implement plan C.

## CLEAN UP

A few select watchers held their meetings in a room attached to a secret passageway under an old factory. They were the key players involved with the case against General Chad Hoskins who now led a guerilla terrorist group, originally created by his father, against his own country. Erica had collected enough data on him early in his career and reported back to the Shadow Organization.

After twenty years, the group would finally act on behalf of the government to remove him. All the agents assembled wore long, dark brown hooded robes concealing their identities in the dank storeroom. A single candle, glowing in the center of the circle they created, cast shadows along the walls. Some knew each other by voice alone, anonymity mostly kept.

The grim atmosphere during the meeting, didn't give Erica any reassurance from her peers regarding her safety and that of her children, although it appeared to be implied.

"All you have to do is get you and your children out." The host explained. "If he shows up before that, you cannot kill him. We need him alive." The tone of his voice did not put her at ease. "Please, you must not worry. We will not intentionally let any harm come to you."

Under the hood, her expression slowly crumbled.

*I'm on my own.*

No matter what they said, she would have to defend her home until rescued or dead. The meeting adjourned after an hour with everyone orating mixed feelings about the entire mission. They dispersed in different directions for security's sake.

As she entered a dark corridor on the second floor, her feet faltered. She let out a squeaky, high-pitched noise then cried. Her anguish spilled out of her, making her unaware of her surroundings.

From behind, she heard the swishing robes of a shadow agent. She had no time to react or protest as he grabbed her shoulders and spun her around, pushing her against a chest table on the wall. He kissed her hard, bruising her lips. She tried to struggle, too weak for a fight, knowing her state of mind. To her amazement, he was twice as strong, even when she gave it her all.

He picked her up with ease and set her on top of the chest table. His hands reached under her robe, ripping her panties off, forcing her legs open. He pressed closer to grasp her buttocks for stability as he plunged inside her. She cried out.

It seemed to not register for him; He didn't care. Her tears were not from pain or rage. They were for the misery she would have to endure a few days from now, her life in shambles. She stopped fighting and resigned to the desperate act.

The shadow man concentrated only on getting Erica's mind off the meeting and everything else being set in motion. He had not planned on taking her this way. Opportunity arose. Ever since training, he always wanted her, and if she were to end up dead in a few days this became his only chance. He had no faith in the organization protecting her, and they forbade him to interfere. Whatever joy she had left, he would give her.

**Three days later**

Hoskins came busting through the front door like a tank and made a beeline for the kitchen. It being early afternoon, all the kids were present from school. He didn't say a word as he entered. Erica rinsed off some vegetables at the sink while the kids made a fuss about setting the table. Their teenage son tossed the plates down in place, making them clank.

His daughter saw him first, giving a big smile. He ignored her and grabbed his wife by the hair and threw her against the wall. The children scrambled out of the way as he flipped the table on its side to get an unobstructed path to her.

Before she could get up, he kicked her hard enough to push her back into the adjacent living room. She coughed up blood and held fast to her abdomen, blocking his next blow. Not to be denied, he took hold of her ankle and forced her body to uncurl. He punched her in the kidney and threw her further into the room.

"You know why this is happening, don't you?" He spat, advancing on her.

She knew it would not end nicely as she lay crumbled in a heap on the floor, choking on her own blood. Her husband meant to kill her. He had good reason to be angry except for the wrong person. His anger should be directed at himself for being so arrogant in his endeavors.

Even though she also worked for the government, Erica didn't turn evidence against him. An agent relayed information regarding the crimes he committed against his country to her in confidence only a few days before the meeting. Once validated, they advised her to remove the children from the home. Too late for that now.

Her eyes cut upward to see how far away he was. His last blow had knocked her across the dining room floor, where she ended up under the table.

Only the table legs behind her came into view.

Still in full dress uniform, Chad came looming over his wife of twenty-one years, eyes filled with hatred. Hell bent on killing her before the extraction team arrived. They both heard helicopters heading toward the house. The team would come through the windows and doors to get him.

Clearly, in her observation, he won't go down without a fight. She saw his focus, at present, bordered on making sure she suffered before then. His fist came down into the side of her face as she turned to look at him.

Without pause, he hit her again, screaming, "You fucking cunt! You're not gonna' live to see past the next hour!"

Their children stood in the kitchen, watching the scene through the dining room doorway as they leaned against the sink. She watched their twelve-year-old daughter stare with eyes full of excitement. Her father had spoiled the girl rotten over the years in a coup to turn her against her own mother. Now she cheered her father on.

"Get her, daddy!" She yelled happily.

Her twin brother, stood next to her, sobbing in despair.

Despite being a dutiful wife, she could have killed him with one blow. Her orders forbade that action, since the government wanted him alive to stand trial. So, she used every bit of her training to not fight back as he kicked and punched while she lay on the floor, protecting her vital body parts. She didn't know how much longer it would last.

Their sixteen-year-old son couldn't take it anymore and came charging into the room to rescue his mother. She had no way of stopping him in her condition. No match for his thirty-year career military trained father, she saw his body fly into the wall beside the doorway from one back-handed blow. She felt nauseous hearing his body hit. Even their young daughter, mesmerized by the brutal assault on her mother, looked uneasy. Her face wrenched in confusion as she suddenly feared for her mother's life.

Erica felt pity and sadness for the girl.

*"It's alright...you don't have to wait long."*

She said to her daughter in her head.

A steady hum of activity outside became a roar as the extraction team came within close proximity of the house, rattling the windows. The cavalry had arrived. Another blow to her ear from her husband's fist muffled the sound, causing enough damage to leave her temporarily deaf.

*Enough.*

Her movements were swift and automatic as she shot up from the floor, grabbing his arm in mid swing for a punch and breaking it in two places. She cracked two of his ribs, broke his nose, and landed a hard blow to the side of his skull. In the few seconds it took to deliver those blows, there also went the last bit of strength she had. Her body went limp and fell back to the floor at the same time her husband dropped unconscious like dead weight.

The extraction team leader, Commander Adam Kroger, came crashing through the windows with his men in tow. Glass sprayed all over the dining room as twenty men, locked and loaded, advanced. More came bursting through the front door, flooding the house. Kroger rushed to the Erica's side to check her vital signs. He turned and saw the General out cold.

"Get her out of here before the second wave shows up!" He barked. He saw the three children still in the house, the oldest down. "Make sure no one talks to them, and they do the same," he commanded two of his men.

While all his orders were being carried out, he went to check the General's pulse. He breathed a sigh of relief.

"She did good." Signaling two of his best men to him, he whispered, "He's still breathing. Bag him and take him to Mercy. No one, and I mean no one, is to get near him but our high security team. You guard his sorry, treacherous ass until they get there. Understood?"

They all stood at attention, saluted, and barked, "Sir, yes sir! Mission accepted!"

Dismissed, they went to task trying to find some way of hauling the General out before he came to.

"Time to punch your meal ticket to hell, General."

Kroger sneered as he looked down at the man's large frame sprawled on the floor.

Outside, neighbors had come out of their homes like cockroaches, rubber necking around each other to see about the commotion. Kroger came out of the front door and frowned. He tapped the commlink behind his ear.

"Where's the national guard? They should have been here already."

"ETA, three minutes, sir. There was traffic."

He rolled his eyes and raised his head up to the sky. Closing his eyes, he let out a deep breath before lowering his gaze back to the street scene. People were already whispering speculations on why an entire military unit had descended on the General's home.

*Thank God we took everyone out through the back of the house.*

The National Guard showed up, burning rubber as they nearly ran over nearby civilians. They jumped out of their vehicles and immediately pushed back the crowds. Yelling out orders for them to return to their homes.

A handful of neighbors became defiant, citing laws prohibiting such rough treatment, and ended up receiving bodily harm. Within fifteen minutes, every civilian was back where they belonged, with armed guards at their doors to prevent leaving.

"Now that we got that under control, we can start clean up," one of his commanders said.

"Make sure not a trace of this is present. And those people keep their mouths shut."

"Roger that."

Kroger turned around and stared at the damage left in their wake. It resembled a drug bust gone horribly wrong. All that was needed to complete the scene were a couple of dead bodies.

*Christ. I'm going to get shit for this.*

The moment they wheeled in the General, the military locked down the entire east wing of Mercy Hospital under protocol. Kroger briefed a limited staff comprising two doctors and four nurses on what they could and could not say or do.

One doctor and two nurses were for the General; the others were for his wife. Towards the end of the east wing, they were setting up a private room for when she got out of surgery. The corridors were quiet as a tomb.

Hoskin's heavily guarded room had no windows or curtains. His injuries treated and his unbroken arm put in a restraint, the nurse sedated him. Erica's surgery would go on for a long while.

Their three youngest children, witnesses to the horror, sat quietly in the waiting room with four armed soldiers as guards, keeping watch. Being there and not knowing any details seemed to be hard for them. They knew their father had gone berserk and tried to kill their mother. That armed soldiers came crashing through the windows and doors.

All three probably felt sick to their stomachs.

The twelve-year-old daughter sat with her knees drawn into her chest, rocking back and forth, still confused by overwhelming feelings. Her twin brother sat slumped down in the seat next to her. The sixteen-year-old leaned against the wall next to them, staring into nothing. He sustained a mild concussion from hitting the wall, being tougher than they thought. If the blow had been any harder, he wouldn't be conscious right now.

Kroger shook his head in pity. The oldest children were being summoned from their assigned stations; their superior officers swore to get them safely back on U.S soil. Word spread fast, and soldiers didn't take too kindly to traitors or their children.

He wasn't too worried about the daughter.

The elder of the kids, she resembled a tower of fury. As a lieutenant in charge of a combat unit, her name was infamous. Her brother, a hothead in contrast, seemed prone to cause trouble. Until their mother could function on her own, they would have to take guardianship over their siblings. He took another look at the younger ones. They were going to have a hard life ahead.

Dr. Sterling, assigned to take charge of Erica's care, sat in a rolling chair by her side in the private room. He took out a piece of chewy candy, removed the wrapper, and slowly put it in his mouth. The balled-up wrapper got shoved into his lab coat pocket as he chewed.

He appeared unaged, still beautiful, with dark wavy hair landing just above his shoulders, dark blue eyes, and full lips. Almost too young for his expertise. Some of his unconventional mannerisms as a surgeon gave him away. No one would have guessed mid-forties.

Watching her sleep, he thought how well she had come out of surgery. Her body was a mess. Any normal person would have been dead long before getting to the hospital.

*What a miserable fucker,* he said to himself, regarding Chad Hoskins.

It would be days before she healed enough to where she could open her eyes. Her injuries were that severe.

On the third day, Hoskins Jr. woke up screaming obscenities, spitting into the face of his former soldiers.

"Where's that fucking cunt of a wife? Is she dead yet? Did I kill that bitch?"

He writhed against his restraints, to no avail. If he had gotten loose, a guard would have to put him back down.

Kroger stood up from his chair across the room and approached his side. He was running out of patience.

"Who the fuck are you?" The disgraced General yelled.

"The last thing you need to add to your crimes, sir, is another murder charge. I think you should pray that she makes a speedy recovery for your sake."

"Puh!" Hoskins Jr. rolled his eyes. "She's about worthless to anyone. How much you give her to spy on me and report back? The beating I gave her better had been worth it."

"Nothing. She didn't give us anything. We told her about the extraction and to remove the children and herself out of the home. Then we told her why. That was only a few days ago, General."

Hoskins Jr.'s face scrunched up in disgust, realizing what it implied.

"You bastards!" He relaxed a bit and said, "Doesn't matter, I'd have killed her anyway, eventually. My family here in the states is unimportant to me."

"That's sad to hear. I doubt you would have killed your wife so easily. Remember, she did this to you."

Kroger motioned his hand across the General's body.

Erica also woke up, screaming in pain. The medication had worn off because the nurse had missed a dosage. Winston tried to calm and restrain her, furious. Once he administered the sedative, she immediately relaxed. He let her go, wiping the tears from her eyes with his index finger.

"It's okay, sweetheart. You're safe here with me."

He stroked her hair as she turned to look at him. He saw something in her eyes register as familiarity, her face contorting when she wasn't sure. She flinched as he reached over to adjust her oxygen line. He smiled a little at her eyes going wide with recognition a split second before she fell back into deep slumber.

An agent of the Shadow Organization, a secret government assassin. Like her

"I'm going to take good care of you."

Winston checked her vitals an hour later and sat back down by the window. It took every part of his being not to touch her while she slept soundly, and. They first met on the training battlefield. He had only known her for three years and didn't see her again for another ten.

In their profession, the organization forbade knowing your associates unless absolutely necessary. Let alone keep track of each other for personal reasons. When he learned about her assignment to the military as a spy to keep the then Commander Hoskins on a leash, it devastated him. He knew then he could never have her.

Then fate brought them together in that dark corridor. She couldn't know his identity then, and he made sure it didn't matter. Once she realized it, he vowed to tell her everything. Until then, he would keep taking care of her for as long as it took.

She stirred at the sound of crashing down the hall. Alarmed, Winston went to look out the door towards the commotion. Turning back, he saw her bolt upright, despite her injuries, hearing her husband's booming voice. He apparently started up again, cursing, fighting, and spitting. Her body shook uncontrollably.

Rushing over to her, he held her in his arms and tried to lay her back down. She resisted for a moment, then clung to him before slipping back into deep sleep. The military shceduled the General's expedition in two days. Until then, he hoped she could manage.

He injected a more powerful sedative, a concoction of his own creation, into her I.V. bag and left to attend another secret meeting.

⬎

Accusations flew as the meeting got underway at a previous venue being used again. The closest and fastest that they could get to with all hell breaking loose in the area. Everyone wanted to know who to blame for the fiasco that took place in the General's home.

A debacle like this put the organization in a poor light. The door burst open in the middle of a heated debate, revealing an enraged man in a gray suit charging down the stairs towards the landing. No one spoke as they realized, in disbelief, he did not wear his robe.

"Is this the kind of organization we are?" He yelled, stopping on the third step from the bottom. "We let one of our own nearly get killed because, heaven forbid, we may save a life instead of taking one this time!"

"You're out of line! This was not our doing!" The host shot back.

"Then you tell me who was supposed to look out for her when the shit hit the fan! Can you tell me that?"

"For god's sake, you're not wearing your robe!"

"I don't need a robe to know who you fuckers are and I don't care if you see me because you all know who I am, anyway!"

The hostility went rampant as everyone in the room threw off their hoods. More accusations and arguments flew freely, raising the decibel levels almost unbearable. The host stopped it when the situation got out of hand with weapons drawn.

"Gentlemen! This is not a bar brawl!" Pointing to the robeless man. "I understand you're upset, we all are, but this is not helping!"

"Someone better fix this and make it right!" The intruder spat as he turned and left out of the room. Silence ensued for a long moment among the attendees. Weapons secured.

The host turned to Winston. "How is she?"

"Completely traumatized. I don't think she can snap out of it in a short time frame. She will have to be decommissioned for a while. Her body is beat all to hell."

"She's been through worse."

"Not like this. Your enemy is one thing. Having your spouse of nearly twenty years try to kill you in front of your children is another matter."

"You will take care of her?"

"Of course," he replied, turning away from the host.

He didn't want anyone to see the look of resentment written all over his face. The whole affair was a travesty in his book.

༺

Chad lay resting his eyes when he felt a presence in the room. Opening them, he looked over the bridge of his nose and saw his twelve-year-old daughter standing at the foot of the hospital bed. She beamed at his awareness of her. He found it repulsive. He never liked her. She bounded over and gave him a big hug.

"Aww, have you come to see daddy? My little despicable wench came to see me. How sweet."

She frowned at that. He could tell she didn't like it.

"Daddy, I came to make sure you were alright."

"Really? Why would I care about a spoiled little bitch that has no respect for her own mother?"

She flinched at his words, tears welling up in her eyes.

"But you said I shouldn't like her, Daddy."

"What kind of daughter treats her own mother like shit just because Daddy said so? You disgust me. My other daughter is only five, and she knows better than that."

She backed out of the room slowly hugging herself.

"Other daughter," she whispered.

He snickered, turning to one of the guards saying, "This is another reason I don't like this damn country. American children are so stupid."

He watched her bolt out of the room sobbing shamelessly. What everyone else knew, she finally came on the verge of learning. It would probably take months before she truly got it. He grunted in satisfaction.

Winston placed his hand on Erica's bare chest to feel her heartbeat as he watched it rise and fall with each breath. His hand slid down into her cleavage, then grazed across her right breast, cupping it slightly as he pulled away before removing his hand from under her gown. She sighed; her head turned from him, the sedative in full swing.

This was wrong, he knew it, yet could not help himself. In his mind, a plan was brewing to take her away from all of this, though it would never work. Even shadow men had some protocol, not to mention the hospital crawling with government agents and soldiers. He remembered how she felt that night and how sweet her mouth tasted.

Aroused, he stopped those thoughts in their tracks.

"I am going to take care of you from now on. They can't stop us this time."

He leaned over and softly kissed her lips. He felt a tingle at the back of his neck alerting him to someone watching. Out of the corner of his eye, he spotted the shadowman turning the corner to the elevators. The white braid down the man's back told the doctor who came to visit.

The Snowman.

～

The next secret meeting involved two people in attendance. The Snowman and an operations agent for the Shadow Organization met to assure General Chad Hoskin's demise. To make sure nothing prevented their ultimate goal. If the General found a way out of the country, the next step would be to hunt him down and dispose of him; discreet and quiet.

The Snowman was the option. Tall and striking, with fair, smooth skin like cream and the facial features of an angel. His lips were just the right shade of pink and his naturally platinum blond hair fell past his waist. He always wore white suits, somehow never seen in a crowd, unless he wanted to be.

That's what disturbed the agent the most. A stealth unlike any human on the planet. The amount of training to master something so devious in nature boggled his mind. The Snowman's current assignment as Marzonetti's private bodyguard was merely a front. This new side project would be under the radar and not affect his role at all, taking only three days.

"I have studied the General for many years and I know he will not go quietly into a courtroom to be tried by the government he betrayed. He has an exit strategy," The Snowman finally said.

The operations agent nodded in agreement. That's why he chose him.

"I figured as much. The moment he gets on any transportation out of the United States, I want you on his tail. Let him settle in at his other home for a day or two, then execute him. We prefer Guerilla style. We want it to look like an enemy from afar did him in."

"Affirmed. You will get a report within seventy-two hours of his death."

As the operations agent left, The Snowman turned into an alley to make a phone call. Time to have a chat with the good doctor about his conduct as of late. Winston needed to find a better way regarding his feelings towards another agent and be more discreet.

"Meet me on the roof by the east wing at 0200 hours."

In the dark of twilight always seemed the best time for serious conversations dealing with life and death. A gust of wind whipped his hair away from the sides of his face. He stood picturesque on the rooftop in an all-white suit with a carnation pink shirt matching the color of his lips. The Snowman knew himself to be a beautiful, extremely dangerous creature molded into an assassin.

Winston hung up his cell phone. He stood at the window in the hospital room watching the rain come down. The Snowman wanted to meet. It had been a long time since they were in the same room together, the last being at a remote location during training.

Those were horrifying days he kept at bay in the dark recesses of his memory. How he survived the torture, stress, and damage inflicted upon his body and mind still amazed him.

Times like these tempted him to pick up smoking again. He wondered if the Snowman sided with him or assigned to dispatch him for breaking protocol. The answer would come soon enough. For now, he had to make sure his ward came out of this mess with some of her sanity intact.

The Snowman stood majestic, shining like a god in the darkness only two in the morning brings. His arms crossed in front of him, he let the breeze flap his long white coat back around his calves. In front of him lay the city in all its glory, viewed from the hospital roof. He did not turn around when he heard the click of the metal door closing, although the fact he did not hear it open he found troubling.

The doctor moved cautiously with every reason to do so. To put the man's mind at ease, Eldan did not reach for his sword, which lay concealed in the folds of his coat.

"The night air is invigorating tonight, don't you think?" His attempt at small talk failed.

"Only if it is the last one you see."

"A bit touchy, aren't you?"

"Why are you here?" Winston asked.

"Don't do anything stupid. There are better ways of getting what you want."

Winston frowned.

*Were my intentions so obvious for the organization to figure out?*

Hoping that was not the case, he moved his hand into his lab coat pocket and gripped the scalpel he had pilfered. He knew the Snowman had seen the gesture.

"Relax, Doctor. I am the only one who knows how you feel. I always knew you had a thing for her when I saw you try to help her in a training session. You would fall for a weapons and hand to hand combat specialist." Eldan sighed. "How nostalgic."

"I'd rather not think about those. If it weren't for

medical science, we would all be dead."

"Thank god for regeneration chambers." Eldan looked down at Winston's hand still in his pocket. "You may be good with a scalpel, but I am much faster than you and better with blades."

"I was going to take a chance either way if it came down to it."

"Don't leave her side. Move into the house with her if you have to. This is not over yet. If the General gets out of the country, he'll send men to finish her off. If he dies, the same happens because they are quite loyal. She can't defend herself right now. How long before she is combat ready?"

"You're joking! It could take at least a year. The damage is that bad. And you don't have to tell me to stay with her. I would have done it regardless of if the organization approved it or not."

"Good. They're not going to fight you on it. The whole thing is a mess. Celestial Mother is furious at how her pets handled this."

"We are also her pets, you know."

"Yes. Although, we are a little more special, don't you think?"

"Well, we are in the top ten."

"Ten? There are only six of us. Do not lump in those underlings who couldn't rise to our level."

"Such arrogance," Winston snorted.

"Remember what the Shadowmen strive for and what I said. Fix her."

With that, Eldan left by scaling down the side of the building. In mere minutes, he landed at street level, walking amongst the pre-dawn masses. The Snowman's agile and unassuming nature despite his appearance still pissed him off.

Winston took his hand out of the pocket, then rested

his elbows on the ledge, taking a deep breath to inhale the cool after rain air. If the encounter had become a fight, he knew he would have lost instantly. The scalpel bluff seemed stupid against someone like the Snowman.

The irony of him being known as The Impaler. Knives and sharp objects were his specialty. He used them in various ways, mostly for torture sanctioned by the government. His surgical skills were unmatched. He looked down at his watch. Time to check on my love.

⌒

Vic sat on the large chair in his receiving room, contemplating what to do for the rest of the day. Eldan would be on loan for the Shadow Organization soon and knew he wanted the two of them to have some alone time. Unlike the others, he rebelled and made it clear to Celestial Mother he would not be her puppet.

After returning home to kill his ruthless father and take over the family, it only took two years to restructure the entire chain of command. The Marzonetti family now had a spot in one of five large crime syndicates running the state.

His oldest son had his own faction within the family. Even he feared him. He occasionally pondered whether a strain of insanity ran in the family bloodline. His awful parenting resulted in the youngest child, Anais, to be psychologically broken. He didn't have the right skills to raise children, and their mother wasn't much better.

"Excuse me, boss," a man's voice broke his reverie.

Vic looked up and saw Bartoni standing patiently at the edge of the carpet. In a three-piece charcoal grey suit, he looked more like a corporate CEO than a mob lieutenant. The only thing that gave it away was the deep expression in his eyes. A memento from being in enemy hands for so long.

"You don't come to me unless there is a problem. Why can't you handle it?"

"Alien drug runners."

Vic winced and sat up straight in his chair.

"Again?"

"The police weren't able to handle it the first time and many of them are too scared to go after it again."

"So, what? It falls on us now?"

"That would be the case. Normally." Vic raised an eyebrow. "The organization has requested we supply clean up for a proposed raid scheduled in the next month."

"For the police?"

"Unofficially."

"And how does this…" Vic asked.

"He's been brought out of cryo to finish the job."

An ill feeling hit Vic's stomach. He leaned forward in sympathy for Damon, the soldier turned hired gun for law enforcement.

"He didn't survive the last time. Why? Why put him through that again?"

"They made him better? A new version of his former self? I don't know. He will be the point person on the operation, and we go in after to make sure no one knows the truth."

"You know, I am really not liking the whole aliens popping up out of nowhere. War is coming, we get it, while having to deal with this mess, too." Vic sat back and sighed.

"How do you want to assemble the team?"

"Use your people. The less people who know, the better. And negotiate to push it out another month. We need more preparation than that."

His right-hand man gave a bow of his head and walked out.

"Fucking man eaters," Vic said with disgust.

Alien drug dealers hiding within society in his territory chafed him.

⌒

The police chief came out of his office, pushing the door hard against the wall as he scanned the officers in the precinct.

"Listen up, turds!"

Damon immediately took offense to that, not saying a word after seeing his partner's warning look. He couldn't stand being a detective under the chief's iron thumb. He foung his last precinct at least tolerable.

"We're having a joint briefing on the drug dealing problem in the eighteenth sector. As you know, there have been a lot of casualties in law enforcement when going against that group of thugs."

Grumblings erupted from the room. Damon went pale. He wasn't prepared for another confrontation with those things yet. And he knew his fellow officers had no idea what they were up against.

"You all I assigned, so no one should be late talking about they didn't know. Our team is riding over at O' six hundred."

With that, he went back into his office, slamming the door shut. Damon glanced at his wrist communicator. Two hours before the meeting. He swung his legs off his desk and sauntered over to his partner. A cup of organic yogurt lay in Inslee's hand and ready to be opened with the edge of the seal pinched tight between two fingers. Damon sighed and plucked it from him.

"I was going to eat that," Inslee protested.

"Yeah." Damon dropped it into the cooler by the desk. "Let's go."

"I'm not hungry!" Inslee said. Damon stood straight, towering over him, and looked down in admonishment.

His lips went into a thin line. "Fine. It's your fault if I don't pass my physical."

"You would pass it regardless. You're not fat by any means." He went and grabbed his long black trench coat. "Besides, you like Italian."

"That's where we're going?" Inslee's horrified expression made him smirk.

"Lots of pasta," Damon replied, smiling.

Inslee got up and put on his uniform jacket.

"I'm going to get fat," he mumbled.

Damon couldn't tell him they were going there so he could anxiety eat. The only way he knew how to squash his fears involved stuffing his face with mass quantities of food. Plus, he needed all the energy he could muster to stay alert during the meeting. If a new plan to take the man-eating drug ring had a chance, he wanted to hear every detail.

They arrived at the other precinct right on time, much to the chief's annoyance. He gave them a hard glare as they sat down among the rest of the team. Around thirty officers and detectives crammed themselves into the small meeting room.

Up front were the leads from the special task force, two federal agents and the police chiefs. The white board behind them glowed and became a holoscreen showing a grid of the city. It zoomed in on a large warehouse in the eighteenth district.

"This, ladies and gentleman, is where our target is doing business these days. The last location burnt to the ground, leaving not a trace or clue behind."

"Our mistake was going in under manned and being ignorant of the situation."

"These ain't your usual run-of-the-mill drug dealers. They fight dirty and do a lot of damage."

"Not sure how or why, but they went after our people with extreme prejudice."

"And now we're going to return the favor."

Triangles and red dots populated the areas around the sector on the holoscreen.

"This is how we're going to take them down."

Damon's eyes bulged in shock. He heard an intake of air nearby and turned to see an officer from the first raid sitting a few feet from him. In full uniform, the officer sat dumbfounded by the information. He too had barely made it out of there alive, and Damon could see him reliving it by his expression.

"That's the plan?" Damon asked, furious. "Go in with more bodies and weapons?"

"Yeah! You got a better one, genius?"

"You're going to get us all killed," the other officer snapped.

"Not if you follow orders."

"Have you told them what happened to the officers who didn't make it?" Damon demanded.

The higher ups fidgeted in front of the room. Finally, the federal agent spoke up.

"Look, we don't need to scare everyone over a simple mission. We get in, apprehend as many as we can, and shut the whole operation down."

"We ain't afraid no drug dealers," a detective from the precinct bellowed.

"Already know most of them are sick fucks and killers."

"That's right," another officer said. "We don't need details. Apprehend my ass. If they coming at us hot, they're getting lead belly."

Shouts of bloodlust followed, and the ones who had seen the previous outcome shook their heads in dismay. This would not end well. Damon thought to himself.

Raid night came with a load of fear, anxiety, and overzealous officers ready to shed blood. Damon sat in the passenger side of the patrol car, watching the horde of cops lock and load. Inslee stared in awe at the massive task force.

"I need you to stay put," he said.

"What are you talking about?" Inslee checked his weapons before stowing them in his holsters. "We have the whole thing mapped out."

Damon turned away from the window and leaned close to him.

"You will stay in this sector and not move from this car. Do you understand me?"

Inslee moved back in terror. Damon could see the tiny glow of blue from his eyes reflected in his. He brushed his cheek with one finger, then got out of the car.

"Be careful," Inslee whispered.

Damon poked his head back through the window.

"Remember what I said."

As he walked off towards the rendezvous point, he scratched his head. Factored into his true mission within the raid, he also had to rid the territory of alien hostiles who could wipe out humans if left unchecked. All the while making sure no one noticed.

Up ahead stood the rest of his team, which included the office jackass and his partner. The jackass gave him a nod and blew a kiss.

*I fucking hate this job.*

## ROAD TO WAR

Right as the judge poised himself to grant an injunction request to have the General expedited, all hell broke loose. Kroger had expected Hoskins' people to come for him at the hospital, so when that didn't happen, he felt confident they were clear.

*We should have been more prepared.*

That went through Kroger's mind as he turned at the sound coming from outside the courthouse window. He watched a missile sailing towards him as if in slow motion. The guerilla soldiers being bold enough to hit a federal building defied comprehension.

"Shit! Everybody down!"

He grabbed hold of the soldier next to him and they both hit the floor hard right when the weapon broke through. The courthouse shook from the missile's impact. Debris flew inward, covering the entire room with thick dust. Smoke billowed up from below as the side of the courtroom crumbled away to reveal the afternoon sky. A large piece of the ceiling dropped, smashing the edge of the bench.

The gavel went flying out the judge's hand as the helicopter moved into position a few feet from the newly created exit. Two armed men leaned out from each side and opened fire into the courtroom. The air filled with the smell of burning metal and vapors swirled.

Rapid fire hit the General's lawyer multiple times along with the bailiff. Kroger made a silent gesture to his men, and they returned fire. A couple of soldiers sitting in the back benches went down before they could move into position.

Stray bullets got the judge, sending him falling backwards behind the bench. Kroger felt the sting in his left arm and rolled away from the hole. Blood splatter covered everything. Cursing his judgement for letting so many inside the courtroom, he crawled closer to the opening and took out the gunman in the rear. From the other side, he saw a tow line tossed into the room.

Hoskins, hiding under a flipped over pew, got to his feet and brushed himself off before walking casually towards it. Taking hold of the line, he hooked it around his waist and let himself be reeled into the helicopter. He stood on the ledge once he made contact and turned to smile at Kroger.

"Sucks when things don't go how you want."

"You son of a bitch!" Kroger yelled.

Hoskins gave him a half ass salute, then the finger before climbing aboard.

Multiple stings pulsated from his body. Kroger checked himself and found bullet wounds in his right leg and abdomen. He had no intention of letting his men see him in agony when the pain showed up within the next few minutes.

*Suck it up, soldier.*

"This is Centaur. We need interception of a bird. Sending coordinates," his second in command spoke into his commlink.

Already too late as he saw it, though worth a shot. Kroger stood up, squeezing the wound in his arm to slow the bleeding. A closed hearing with only ten civilians present gave him mild consolation.

Half were down, at least two dead.

"Fuck!"

*How am I going to explain this to General Perrara?*

⌒

With his hands gripping the edge of his desk, General Perrara listened to the report with gritted teeth. The interception attempt proved an epic failure as the enemy rocket launcher shot down the aircraft in pursuit at close range.

Doing anything further would raise suspicion, so he forced his team to let Hoskins escape like his father before him. Administrators from the Department of Homeland Security already cursed his name for losing a multimillion dollar asset.

He slammed a fist down, then stood up straight. This wasn't over yet. Hoskins had a rendezvous point somewhere between Canada and the next country over. A strategy came to him, and he grinned. If he couldn't get Hoskins on American soil, then he would send the fight to the guerilla base.

Of the options for who to send, he thought the Shadowman might be too much. It had to be done quick, silent; down and dirty. He also wanted the man to suffer, so rummaged his mind for another solution. He didn't relish in asking the female alien who the staff started calling Celestial Mother. She was dangerous.

Over the years, he saw the alien trainers take an iron grip on the reigns of new soldiers. His faction no longer had a say in what modules to send trainees through. He crossed his arms as he stared out his office window.

*It's still my baby.*

They could not just shut him out completely. All he needed was one small unit of agents to get the job done. No harm in that.

Celestial Mother sat patiently on her floating platform, waiting for the military representative to speak. She already knew what he wanted and smiled inwardly at his cowardice to ask directly. News of the debacle with the younger Hoskins had spread wide.

*How incompetent can these humans be?* She asked herself.

"Speak, human," she demanded.

The officer's uncertainty became a glare as he looked up at her. His demeanor changed, he stood straighter. His circle respected him, and the indignation showed.

"We do not ask this lightly," he paused, then spat out, "Celestial Mother." A cocky grin formed. "The situation calls for immediate action and currently, our branch cannot have a hand in it."

"Oh? You were doing so well. The Shadowmen are up to speed."

"It should look random, not like an obvious hit."

"Which it surely is," she cut him off. She glared back, looking down on him and returned the same cocky grin. "Denied."

The officer reared back in anger. His hands clenched into fists at his side.

"The reason?"

"Simple. It is a waste of resources. And both Generals will come in handy later in the frame of this war. A necessary anomaly, if you will."

"You can't be serious?" His eyes went wide.

Celestial Mother stood, stepping off her platform, to descend a few inches before him. He had to raise his head until it almost tilted to the ceiling. Fear gripped him. She liked that expression on him better.

"I do not joke about sending my new human offspring out into the field to clean up your messes. They are being trained for war, not domestic disputes. It seems your organization has lost sight of that."

"You want us to leave those two loose ends to sabotage us at every turn?"

She smirked.

"They are of no real threat. When the time comes, both father and son will see the foolishness of their plans and will bend to the circumstance at hand."

"General Perrara," the officer began.

"Would be wise to heed my suggestion."

The discussion over, she leaped silently back onto her platform and settled in. The officer gave a curt salute and pivoted towards the door. He marched out stiffly, never looking back. Once the doors slid closed, Celestial Mother's face scrunched in irritation. Seeing everything unravel on the human side, her counterparts had already discussed a contingency plan in case it went too far.

"When will you learn, humans? It's not about who's right or wrong."

*It's about survival of the fittest.*

⌒

Hot jungle air made hazy waves in front of the Snowman while he laid flat on the grassy knoll, peering through his ocular enhancers. Below him lay the guerilla camp disguised as a small village run by Hoskins Jr. The man himself roamed around, his little girl in tow.

She smiled up at him, and he beamed back with admiration. Her smooth brown skin in stark contrast to his paleness, and sandy colored hair gave away her mixed blood. In her arms, she carried one of the newer assault rifles. Smaller, lightweight, but three times as deadly and she knew how to use too.

The Snowman tapped the side of the viewer to disable it, then slinked backwards into the brush. The agent dispatched him to locate the General and stand by for the kill team. Not twenty minutes ago, they relayed a stand down command.

Now, he collected intel for future reference. None of this surprised him. Being in the jungle, in his opinion, seemed a waste of his talents.

And for what?

A narcissistic jackass with no understanding of the war ahead. His commlink beeped loudly, and he stared at it in horror. Something within the perimeter had triggered its frequency. By the sound decibel, he feared the worst and cursed softly.

He reactivated his viewer in time to see a big guy in a light-colored suit and white t-shirt staring directly at him from the village's communal dining area. The man gave a sinister smile before going up to whisper in Hoskins Jr.'s ear. At first the former General became enraged, then nodded and waved the man away.

*Oh, shit!*

Sure enough, the man came charging towards him at inhuman speed. A Terror. The only thing on par with Shadowmen. And not just any kind. This one didn't care about which side paid him, or humanity even. Its only objective, to kill. The Snowman shut off the viewer and jumped down to meet his foe. The option to run not in the cards. They clashed in midair, landing a few feet from each other.

A slight raised line above the Terror's clavicle darkened, and the Snowman cursed silently. He thought he had cut deep enough to sever his neck at least part way, stopping the attack. This Terror had fortified skin.

The Snowman didn't have his sword with him on this mission. He could have easily sliced through rock, let alone this guy, if he had. Standing in a defensive stance with his short blade, he waited.

The man touched the cut and smiled.

Whipping off his jacket exposed well-defined arm muscles. Snowman braced himself for a grueling fight.

"Shadow," the Terror whispered.

Before the Snowman could react, the man came at him. They sparred at lightning speeds; the Snowman blocking most of the blows. The Terror grabbed hold of his leg and lifted him upside down, ready to throw him to the ground. The Snowman countered by turning his body around to grab his in return.

The Terror let go right before he went on his back as the Snowman landed on his feet a yard away. He could feel stings along his arms and legs, a sign of bleeding. For the first time, he noticed the Terror's fingernails, now talons extended a good three inches. Thin, sharp and stained red from the wounds they inflicted.

*Stupid! I should have noticed that sooner.*

The Terror wasted no time in resuming his assault, talons positioned to pierce his opponent's midsection. The Snowman brought down his forearm to block them and used the man's shoulder as a launch pad in anticipation of the second taloned hand coming up towards his chin. He felt it graze the side of his face as he cleared the distance.

Without hesitation, the Terror turned and swiped his abdomen. Again, the Snowman barely evaded the hit, feeling the sting. For a brief second, their eyes connected, and the Snowman saw what lie beneath. Madness. Sheer murderous intent with the only reason being enjoyment.

*I'm in trouble.*

He had been in many life-or-death situations, fighting enemies with convictions. A collective goal or purpose in mind. This one had none. If those talons got to him, they would rip his heart out of his chest before he realized he was dead.

And he wasn't dying today.

A quick scan of his surroundings found an opening back towards the rendezvous point. He would have to rival the Terror's speed and it would burn him out fast.

As if reading his mind, the Terror maneuvered into his line of sight and leaped into the air, spinning fast with talons out. They resembled a rotary saw at full speed. Cartwheeling backwards would do more harm than good, so the Snowman dropped and slid beneath him.

The Terror switched position midway and one of his talons cut through his shoulder. Clenching his teeth so he wouldn't scream out in pain, the Snowman rolled on his side onto his feet. Within a heartbeat, he took off in the opposite direction towards his drop point, the Terror right behind him.

As the Terror gained on him, a loud screech erupted. The Terror stopped dead in his tracks. Thanking the Gods for a small miracle, the Snowman continued at top speed. He reached the edge of the cliff and took a deep dive into the canyon. Closer to the ground, a stealth bird waited for him. The top opened as he crashed down hard into it; the cushion doing little good. Blood flew from his mouth when he landed on his back. He watched the hatch close and felt the aircraft lift off as he lost consciousness.

*Fuck! I lost!* Was his final thought.

Hoskins Jr. sat under the wooden structure that blocked the sun. The communal eatery resembled a picnic area with benches and tables. He saw his Terror come back to the village, picking up his jacket on the way and donning it. There were a few white scratches on his neck and arms.

Hoskins snorted.

His father was right. Those Shadowmen were not all that great against a Terror. Especially his. He had called the thing back because he felt no need to prove that fact. For the Shadowman to feel defeat was enough.

"Good job, Renno." That being his name, many called him Rhino for good reason. "Come cool off and have a drink."

"Yes, boss." Renno sat down at the end of the table.

"Rhino awesome!" His daughter cried out.

A soldier in full camo gear and a rifle slung across his shoulder set a glass of iced tea in front of him. As he took a sip, Hoskins eyed the thing.

"So, what did you think of that Shadowman?"

Renno gulped half the glass and set it back down. "Dangerous."

"But you bested him. He can't be that strong."

Renno frowned into his glass, twirling it slowly.

"He didn't go all out."

Renno's expression turned dark, and rage consumed the man. By not giving his all, the Shadowman had disrespected the Terror. Hoskins, too, felt a bit upset by this. If you're going to commit to a fight, do it one hundred percent. Then a revelation hit him. If that Shadow halfassed it, what were the Shadowmen really capable of?

The desert base medical bay doors opened for the military crew scrambling down the ramp. On the floating stretcher, the Snowman lay bloody and unconscious. From the platform above, Hana sucked in a hard breath. He knew the four aliens would be livid if they saw him.

A smart phone, tossed by one of the soldiers escorting the stretcher, came towards him and he caught it. The notification light blinked, with the name Boss shining bright. Reluctantly, Hana hit the call icon.

"Where are you?" Vic Marzonetti's voice demanded. When he didn't get an answer, his voice changed.

"This isn't him. Who is this?" Vic's rage came through.

Hana took a deep breath.

"I need you to calm down."

"I'll kill every last one of you if he dies!"

"Yes, you've threatened us with that before."

"It's not a threat." Marzonetti went silent for a moment. "Tell me."

"You know I can't do that. He's going to be fine. We will send him back in a week or so."

"I'll be waiting."

The line went dead, and Hana let out a sigh of relief that became short-lived. As he headed into the viewing deck of the surgical theatre, Karias rounded the corner. The alien stopped halfway down the hall and stared into the room as the door shut.

*Oh, goddamn!*

Sure enough, the door opened back up and he came in to stand next to Hana. He looked down into the operating room where doctors cut off the Snowman's clothes to attach the electrodes to his body in preparation for the regeneration chamber.

"Why is one of my pupils in such ragged condition?"

"Secret mission?" Hana replied, cringing.

"Secret as in defying our wishes?"

"We did not defy your wishes!" Hana said curtly. "He was on surveillance only."

"Yet, here he is. Near death."

Hana had never seen blood on the Snowman. With so much in the man's platinum hair and on his pale, creamy skin, it disturbed him. It angered him as well. That would have to wait. Movement out of the corner of his eye made him turn to see Karias leaving. They couldn't keep celestial Mother in the dark much longer.

Once again, General Rubio Perrara found himself at a crossroads. The last time he had to summon up mass amounts of courage he informed his father that the organization no longer deemed his role necessary. To this day, they never talk about it, knowing it to be the right thing to do.

That came after Professor Makoto left feeling betrayed and bitter,. He apparently expected Hana to remain only his and balked at the thought of his prized possession being impregnated by some lowly soldier. He had to restrain the professor when he slapped Hana so hard, the young man fell back and went to deliver another blow.

His father condoned Makoto's actions. He couldn't stand for it. Hana's value surpassed both of theirs combined.

Now, he made his way to see the alien trainers and personally confront Celestial Mother. No reason to make her an enemy. He wanted to reassure her they would in agreement on protocols hence forth. The female alien scared him to death and not because of her height. Her malice towards humans stemmed from something Hana had said or done by the way she watched the tragically beautiful man. Like a lioness protecting her cub.

He swiped his keycard on the elevator panel and waited for it to arrive. The ride down, he took a few deep breaths to get his mind right. As soon as the doors opened to the communal room, he straightened his shoulders and marched in.

The four aliens turned their attention to him. His flesh felt clammy, and invisible ants crawled along every inch of his skin.

"Good afternoon. I came personally to speak with you all about our agenda moving forward." He realized he had said it too fast and took another breath.

"Relax, General," Celestial Mother said. "Please, sit down. You look pale."

"Thank you." Perrara went to an empty chair.

"You think I have no understanding of the human psyche?" She cocked her head.

"That's not true," he replied. "I think you probably know more about us than we do."

"Is that so? Then why the rebellious antics?"

"Humans are stubborn?" He answered.

"No. It's your arrogance. With all that has happened over the past decades, your kind still clings to outdated thinking and practices. What are you afraid of?"

General Perrara swallowed hard and thought about it. Churches were popping up again after twenty years of being defunct. Frustrated humans, angry at the rapid evolution, took up arms to eradicate aliens, forgetting that it would do more harm than good when the enemy arrived. All of it was irrational behavior.

"Many humans feel frightened whenever there is a big shift in the world. Fear of the unknown. We tend to go back to basics instead of looking ahead."

"Then why should we commit any more time to saving you?" Her mate asked.

"Because," Perrara said adamantly, "despite those anomalies, most of mankind wants to survive. I am asking you to believe in our will."

Celestial Mother crossed one arm, raising the other at a ninety-degree angle. Her fingers toyed with a few strands of hair. A very human act, Perrara thought. They had been here long enough for certain traits to rub off on them.

The aliens glanced at each other, and a silent nego-tiation took place. General Perrara got up and poured himself a glass of water from the dispenser. The one thing they kept specifically for humans who came to visit.

He gulped down the entire glassful.

His skin returned to feeling normal.

"We shall continue," the bigger Chombrazen, Karias, finally said.

General Perrara set the glass down and stood.

"I am forever grateful. Thank you."

"You are more in tune with the world compared to your father. I am impressed." Celestial Mother's platform descended before him, and she reached out to brush his cheek. "Go. Worry not."

He walked back to the elevator and boarded. On the way up to the main level, he shivered. The gleam in her eyes told him plenty. They were continuing to give aid for their own agenda, not for the sake of humanity. Surviving the upcoming war would be a testament to how far humans could evolve into a species worthy of being included in the galaxy.

The question arose on how the organization could safeguard their recruitment pool to achieve that goal. A new plan slithered its way into his thinking and a frown formed. It wasn't ideal, but if push came to shove, he would use it. The survival of mankind depended on drastic measures now more than ever.

\*\*END\*\*

EXCERPT FROM

CURVE OF HUMANITY
BOOK THREE

PURGE SEQUENCE

## ESTABLISHED LAWS

Hana hated bureaucracy despite its necessity. Six representatives sat in his conference room looking bent out of shape about Bi-Genetics being taken out of their environment or homes without consulting the protective agencies put in place at the height of the facilities.

He snorted out loud, getting their attention for the wrong reasons. Those government entities protected no one. All a sham, in his opinion. More sin and atrocity happened in those places than anywhere else.

The Child and Welfare representative cleared her throat. Hana gave her an evil look and the woman flinched before speaking.

"There was an incident in Indiana that we cannot condone. The family was physically assaulted to the point of being incapacitated and the child was drugged before removed."

Hana's eyebrows shot up. "Oh?"

"This is not a laughing matter," the Family Advocate rep spat. His forehead was scrunched, face turning pink.

"Is there any proof of this alleged drugging and what not?" Hana asked playfully.

The other reps went rigid in their seats admonishing her lack of seriousness.

"The father happened to see the needle being stuck in as he lost consciousness."

"So," Hana cooed. "You want to take the word of a

man who imprisoned his twelve-year-old son and broke multiple bones in his body as well?

They all frowned with acknowledgement. Condemning his organization for one thing , yet not calling out the people doing these crimes against Bi-Genetics set a new low.

"We're not saying we agree with what the parents had done. Your people didn't even give us a chance to try and remedy the situation."

"Let me guess. Family counseling, maybe a short stay in foster care before sending him right back into that house, or maybe you would just do a monthly check in?"

The Health and Human Services rep slammed his fist on the table.

"We are not monsters! We are doing what we can!"

"Without falling out of favor in the public eye. It's no secret how many of the population feel about my kind."

"We need to work together, or this won't get fixed," the Child Welfare rep said.

Hana endured another hour of bantering back and forth, accusations flying, until everyone was thoroughly fed up with each other and left one by one. Sighing with relief, he tapped his tablet's commlink and opened the messenger. He found the recipient he wanted and typed two words.

*Good job.*

Back in his newly renovated office, Hana tossed the tablet down on the desk and slid into the chair. He let his head fall back while closing his eyes. All he wanted to do right now was not think about anything. Being a part of the Shadow Organization started off as a great idea. Now he had doubts.

A swishing sound from the hall made him perk up and lean forward.

The bigger Chombrazen alien, Karias, stood in the

doorway wearing his layers of robes that dragged on the floor. His body took up the entire frame, blocking light from coming in the room. Those golden eyes always full of malice peered down on him.

"Did your meeting go well?"

Hana cleared the lump in his throat.

"Of course not. Everyone is being stubborn or clueless."

"What did you expect?"

The alien seemed genuinely curious.

"I'm not sure. Maybe some sense of moving forward. A new era of tolerance for a diverse civilization." Hana frowned at his own words.

The alien burst out laughing, his voice a sonic boom localized within the section. Hana heard things dropping and people yelping in fright from the onslaught. When he was done, the alien once again gazed at him.

"I have studied your kinds' history and I see nothing of the sort. Even in the United States, it took over half a century for them to acknowledge their females and those of other ethnic descent. Other countries still did not do so during the time after that."

"Not all of us think that way. It's a few bad apples spoiling the whole bunch."

"Wrong." The alien's word made Hana flinch. "It has always been the opposite."

Hana knew that, yet it still hurt all the same. The top heads in the organization perused his proposal to mirror a plan similar to Ortega City, Metropolis. Including the alien trainers brought in to help humanity be on equal footing with the enemy.

"Your plan is flawed the same way your race is," Karias continued. "In order for it to succeed, humans would need to change how their minds work entirely."

"Then what do you suggest?" Hana asked heatedly.

The alien scoffed and turned to leave.

"Focus on survival. Maybe after humanity is nearly destroyed, the masses will understand."

As he made his way down the hall towards the training entrance, people hugged the walls to give him a wide enough berth. His head almost touched the ceiling.

Hana waited until the alien was nowhere in sight and relaxed back in his chair. The picture slideshow on his desk showed various ones of his family. It seemed like only a while ago that he had been tethered to Professor Makoto. A sting filled his head.

When he no longer needed the old man's affection or approval, a sense of animosity towards him was spawned. He treated Hana like a disloyal servant, a spoiled child, and sometimes lashed out in anger. Even the first General Perrara fell into the same way of thinking, calling him ungrateful after all the Professor had done for him. Hana had firsthand knowledge of how Professor Makoto operated. Those feelings of guilt for running his facility the way he did weren't sincere.

A knock on the door frame made him look up to see his husband, Scott, leaning against it.

"Lost in thought?"

Hana dropped his head in his hands, covering his face. The tears came so suddenly that it shocked him into gasping. Scott came in and folded his arms around him.

"It's going to be okay. Maybe not now, but in the end. You'll see."

"I'm trying the best I can," Hana cried.

Those arms got tighter, and Hana melted into them. He wasn't trying to change the entire world on his own. Merely inject the catalyst for it.

# ABOUT THE AUTHOR

Hi there. I'm Maquel A. Jacob. I have had a passion for the written word since the age of seven, reading everything I could get my grubby little hands on which included encyclopedias and the thesaurus. At twelve, I had my first encounter with a Stephen King novel and was hooked. I then became inspired to write my own brand of fiction. Combining multiple genres to keep things interesting.

I am a HUGE Anime fan, love a great bottle of wine and rock out to heavy metal music. Green and lush Oregon is where I currently reside spinning imaginary worlds in my head and daydreaming.

For cool limited-edition Swag, updates, FREE short stories, Newsletters

...and more

Visit: http://www.maquelajacob.com/

**Become a Patron:**

https://www.patreon.com/maquelajacob

Like Maquel A. Jacob on Facebook

Follow on X (FormerlyTwitter) @MaquelAJ1

Also find me on Goodreads

MAJart Works on Instagram

**For chapter insights, check out my YouTube channel**

https://www.youtube.com/maquelsmusings733

www.ingramcontent.com/pod-product-compliance
Lightning Source LLC
Chambersburg PA
CBHW021012120726
47905CB00009B/2973